# REACHING FOR TOMORROW

## Ros Rendle

SAPERE
BOOKS

# REACHING FOR TOMORROW

Published by Sapere Books.

20 Windermere Drive, Leeds, England, LS17 7UZ,
United Kingdom

saperebooks.com

ISBN: 978-1-80055-689-8

# PROLOGUE

## 2007

Jen leaned over to retrieve one of her pillows from the floor. Somewhere among this tangled bedding was her iPhone. Where was it? She shoved back the covers and rummaged down the bed. Finding it, she turned it off with a sigh. Listening to music wasn't working anyway. She glanced at the open book on the bedside cabinet and turned away, before plumping up the pillows with her fists and flinging herself back down. She turned yet again. The digital clock moved on painfully slowly as she lay and watched the numbers. Her eyes stung and itched, but still they would not close.

Lying on her side, she looked at the pillow next to hers and remembered the indentation she had noted that day all those months ago. In her mind's eye, she saw Mike's tanned back, his broad shoulders. His hair curled down onto his neck, thick and lustrous and as he turned to her his eyes opened and he lifted his hand to rub his face. She loved his hands. His fingers were long and strong with fine, clean nails. The palms were broad and the backs were suntanned. The dark hairs on his chest snuck down...

She screwed her eyes shut and when she opened them again, the image was gone.

*Right*, she thought. *Count to one hundred without moving.* Yet another minute passed. *I know, you're supposed to mentally put things in folders and shut them in a drawer.* The clock changed again.

Why did this have to be happening to her in August? This was supposed to be her period of relaxation, not a time for life-changing decisions. Only five years had passed since Jen had left university to start her teaching career. The passing of time wasn't a consideration then. Right now, she was too worn down to think about that.

She glanced at the clock for the thousandth time and decided she might as well get up, even though it was still early.

The day ahead and the meeting she'd set up with Mike seemed impossible after the months of anguish, as well as all the treatment more recently. It all came down to this single morning.

*I wonder what he's doing right now. Is he pacing? Is he lying in and having sweet dreams of a new life ahead? Is he getting ready?* She pictured Mike's long legs as she remembered them, striding through to the bathroom — toned and tanned from all the running practice. She thought of the rounded muscles of his backside, then puffed her cheeks and blew out.

She grabbed the TV controls before she could imagine more and idly flicked through the channels.

"It's Lammas Day today," said the jolly Breakfast Show presenter. "Now, you lovely ladies and amorous men, in ancient times this was traditionally a day for foretelling marriages and trying out partners for eleven days before deciding whether to go with it or part forever. Probably not recommended for today, though." He laughed.

Jen turned off the set and grunted at it. What was that all about? What a time to be making this decision about her own marriage. She wasn't meeting Mike until eleven o'clock, but she decided she might as well push back the covers and haul herself up.

The shower flowed until piping hot, cascading over her skin. She stood for longer than usual, trying to wash away all her tiredness and indecision. Then she towelled herself dry and threw on her dressing gown.

When she returned to the bedroom to dry her hair and choose the all-important outfit, she looked around her. She liked this room. Despite the tears that she'd shed into the pillow, she'd had moments of contentment too, more recently. When she had first arranged it all, it was to be an ocean of white and blue, calming and serene. She took a deep breath.

Flinging open the wardrobe door, she ran her eyes over the contents. What to wear? Something informal but smart — nothing too schoolish, though; that wouldn't help the atmosphere at all. Still, not too casual either. *I've got some pride left. I'll look confident, even if I don't feel it,* she thought.

Had she been too set in her ways to allow Mike to properly feature in her plans? She genuinely didn't think so. He'd said it was a good idea to apply to her present school after three years in her first job. It was closer to home, so less petrol money meant a small increase in funds, and they'd needed every penny back then. She liked the school, the head seemed good and most of the staff were really friendly. Her promotion there had come in good time too. Was that when it had all started to go wrong at home, though?

Jen moved to the window, where the blue and grey fabric which framed it matched the cornflower colour of the wall behind the bed. For most of the day, the sun brightened this room. She never closed the curtains at night, either. When sleep eluded her, she liked to watch the stars. There was something consoling in their constancy.

She opened the window. The fresh air washed in, and she closed her eyes to feel the full benefit. It was a real sapphire and gold morning. Looking down on the garden, she saw that the wide flowerbed she'd created against the neighbour's fence was a riot of colour. Only a casual gardener, she managed to use fertilizer and to cut off dead heads, but here she had surpassed herself, having planted spring bulbs followed by perennials. Now a plethora of black-eyed Susan, phlox, and salvia greeted her. Then she spotted the day lily. *Here today and gone tomorrow,* she thought morosely. She drew herself up, putting back her shoulders.

The smell of the garden on the warm morning air was heady and delicious. *Whatever happens later,* she thought, *it will be the right thing; for me, at any rate.* She wasn't being selfish — this was self-preservation. Jen had tried living her life just to please. Now, she realised that while compromise was often necessary, giving all she had to someone else was not always for the best.

Drying her hair with care, Jen faced the mirror. The light from the window emphasised the auburn tints that enlivened the brown. She turned to the wardrobe and unhooked the red blouse and the black A-line skirt she'd bought recently, in a fit of mutiny. Then she took down the blue flowered dress that her mum said brought out the colour of her eyes. Really, she'd known all along that it would be the dress. Putting it on, she pulled the tie at the back into a bow. The colour was vibrant but not aggressive. Turning this way and that and craning her neck to see her reflection, she hoped the drawing in of the waist suited her slender figure. She opened the lid of her jewellery box and pored over the contents. Eventually she chose a fine silver necklace and some plain silver studs for her ears, which emphasised her new tidy haircut and slim neck. She had a few good pieces of jewellery, but they all seemed to hold one memory or another. There was the bracelet Mike had bought for their first wedding anniversary, and the gold choker they'd chosen together on holiday. The ring he'd given her when she'd started her first job glared up at her.

She spread her hands and looked at the backs. She didn't wear nail varnish. Her job in the classroom wasn't suited to that at all, and anyway she really couldn't be bothered with all that palaver every other day. Only her wedding ring still encircled her finger. Why did she still wear it? She frowned and shrugged.

A simple pair of flat grey sandals, each with three small diamantes on the front, completed her outfit. She glanced at her watch. It was still only eight thirty. As she surveyed herself in the long mirror, Jen hoped for the correct effect — she wanted to feel confident enough to make her decision, and then determined enough to carry it through. She was still undecided, but she knew something would need to be done. She couldn't go on like this.

She was mooching around restlessly into the living room; back to the kitchen; casually stroking her cat Fudge's head, who started purring; wondering what to do. One day, more than a year ago, just when she'd needed something to care for in her life, Fudge had adopted her as quite a young kitten. Jen had asked around the neighbours and finally visited the vet for all the necessities. Fudge had determinedly made her home with her.

The phone rang. "I bet that's Mum," Jen said aloud to the cat. "Oh, Fudge! I really don't know if I can cope with this call right now." As she lifted the phone, Jen took a deep breath. "Hello."

"How are you doing?" came the reply. It was her friend Pat.

"Oh, Pat. Thanks so much for ringing. I thought it might've been Mum, and I'm not sure I can deal with that right now. I know that's mean."

"I can understand. Maybe you have to look to your own needs today of all days, rather than hers. I'm sure she'll tell you she understands when you next call her," said Pat. "Are you nearly ready?"

"I *am* ready and kicking my heels now, wondering how to kill the time."

"Come up for a quick cup of tea, if you want. Both boys are out on their bikes already, so it'll be just us."

"Thanks, Pat. You read my mind. You're a great friend. I'll be there in two minutes."

Gratefully, Jen grabbed her bag, keys and a cardigan. Pulling the door shut behind her, she ran into the sunshine and hurried up the road to her friend's house.

Pat lived in a small semi, very similar to her own, but there were four of them living there now and it was crowded. The two boys were growing very quickly. Jen raised her hand to knock just as the door opened. Pat had anticipated her arrival and gave her a warm, smiling welcome.

They had first met the day that Jen and Mike had moved in, five years ago. Anticipating their need for coffee, Pat had appeared from up the road with a tray of everything they could want. They had shared half an hour of chatting and drinking and then, ever sensitive, she had left them to get on. Although she was ten years older and further along in terms of family responsibilities, Pat had been a steadfast friend to Jen since that day. Her warmth and understanding had been invaluable. She seemed to know intuitively when to ask and when to listen.

"So…" said Pat, leaving the conversation hanging as they moved towards the kitchen. Jen knew Pat was a ready listener, but she was equally content to wait in companionable silence until Jen was ready. Right now, the kettle was hissing. More often than not, they sat at the table in the kitchen. It seemed the right place to be, among the slight chaos, rather than in the living room where the sofa and chairs meant they were less intimate in their chatter. Frequently the children were in the other room too, watching television or playing games.

Jen sat and glanced around as Pat poured the tea. Everything was as it should be. Ben's and Joe's school art was on the wall next to a large, mounted plate. Empty cake tins were draining next to the sink, and a fruit dish overflowed with oranges. It didn't matter about the clutter; it was right. There was always a homely smell in Pat's kitchen too. Today it was toast rather than bacon.

"I've been like a cat on the proverbial tin roof." Jen smiled, feeling self-conscious.

"Well, you look lovely. Just right."

"Thanks." Jen was relieved. "I've lain awake half the night wondering what to wear, what to say, whether to be five minutes late or to arrive before he does, so I can arrange myself artfully on a bench." She laughed half-heartedly.

"It's the country park, right?" asked Pat as she parked her comfortable frame onto a kitchen chair and put a mug of tea before each of them.

"Yes, it seemed like neutral territory. We didn't want to meet in a pub where everyone can hear what's going on. A restaurant's out in case one of us wants to leave before we've finished eating, and how do you manage the money? That could be very awkward. It's just as well it's good weather, though. Doing this, walking about in the rain, would be far too dramatic, not to say uncomfortable. Who would sit in whose car if we just stayed in the car park? It's a territory thing, isn't it?" Jen realised she was gabbling.

"Well, it seems the perfect place and yes, the weather has come up trumps for once," agreed Pat.

They sipped their tea in silence for a minute.

"So, how is everyone here?" asked Jen, thinking to move away from the subject of herself for a while.

"Oh, we're all fine. The boys are loving the escape from school so far, and as it's early days so I'm not having to invent activities yet. Doug may take them swimming tomorrow, though. He's busy, of course. As it's holidays, he's got all the summer activities on top of the regular stuff. He's short of a lifeguard, so he's doing a bit extra there, too."

Pat's husband, Doug, was a manager at the local leisure centre. Mike and the others always teased him about combing his hair at every opportunity, and it seemed that he couldn't pass a mirror or shop window without checking his reflection. However, they had been friends since that first week. Mike and Doug still got on well, and with Diana and her partner, Greg, who were also friends of Pat and Doug's, they had been a constant 'sixsome' for several years. They'd gone out for the occasional meal, but more often shared an evening in playing a boardgame with a couple of bottles of wine. That way, Pat and Doug didn't need to get a babysitter. It was all different now, of course.

"And what about you?" asked Jen. "You don't look quite so tired."

"I'm more in a routine again," Pat replied. "I'm feeling a bit more relaxed these days." She paused as she seemed to evaluate what she had just said. Then she added, "Well, I've decided to rein in my emotions and be more independent. Marriage is not all it's cracked up to be, for me, anyway, and I'm no longer relying on it. Everyone's different, of course. Don't let my circumstances influence you, Jen. Whatever you decide will be right for you, you'll see."

It all sounded a bit lonely and loveless to Jen.

"There are times when the boys are bickering or something like that and I get wound up, but overall it's fine. Having Doug back here helps then. I get some time to do my own thing when he takes them out for the odd day here and there. That was part of the bargain when he came back. I love them to bits, but being a single parent was draining. In the holidays, Mum sometimes has them, as you know. I'm more self-reliant; I know that I can't rely on Doug anymore. I'm not looking for more these days."

"Do you feel lonely, though?" Jen asked.

"Not really. I have some companionship while he's here that I didn't have when I was on my own for that while. I don't believe in the myths of marriage anymore, and so I shan't be disappointed another time. It's a relief, to be honest, to know where I stand. I know who comes first with Doug, and that's Doug. I feel more self-confident, and I know that I could cope on my own. As it is, the boys have a father and know nothing of what's gone on."

Jen made an effort to wipe away her frown. It all sounded so sad. She changed tack again. "How is your mum?"

"She's great and she's so helpful. To be honest it's given her a new lease of life, since Dad died, to be with the boys more, and she's always got something up her sleeve to help entertain them. She's coming down next week to stay for a while, so you'll see her then. Your mum will be there for you too, you know, if and when you need her," Pat reminded Jen.

"I know, but I can't help feeling Dad prefers her there. She's in the background, though, and that's good. I don't know what I would do without you. I'm so lucky we met, Pat."

"Me too." Pat laughed wryly.

"Well, I'd better think about going," Jen said reluctantly. "Oh Lord! What am I going to do?" She panicked, her voice rising.

"Whoa, Jen. Take a deep breath. You'll be fine. Even if you don't know this minute, I promise, you will when you get there."

Jen's voice ascended again in her anxiety. "Why did this happen to us? It wasn't meant to be like this. What did I do wrong?"

"Who says you did? It's complicated, isn't it? It really is not that simple. There's several of you involved in this, and you each have a view and a part. When you get back, I *will* be here. Just go slowly and drive carefully, for goodness' sake."

"Oh, Pat, thank you," Jen said.

She stood to leave, thinking again how lucky she was to have this friend, so calm and competent. She knew Pat had her moments too, and she'd been there for her at those times, but she doubted she had been so wise and steady.

At the front door, she impulsively planted a light kiss on Pat's cheek. Theirs had not been that sort of demonstrative friendship, and tears sprang to Pat's eyes.

"Go now," she said. "Take care."

Jen turned to wave at the end of the path and retraced her steps towards her own home and her car. She got in and stayed still for several moments, calming her racing thoughts and breathing deeply.

She couldn't delay any longer. She'd drive slowly and maybe stroll in the park before arriving at the bench next to the lake.

The little car was one of Jen's favourite things. It gave her independence and freedom. She turned up the music and let the smooth tones of her favourite singer wash around her. She wound down the window and felt the warm breeze sweep over her face as she drove.

Arriving at the park, she swung her legs out of the car reluctantly. Mothers had brought their children to use the swings and climbing frames. One baby didn't like the swing and was crying loudly. She could hear the calls and shrieks of excitement from others. Two little girls were racing each other towards the playhouse and its slide. She knew some would have brought picnics, too. It was a perfect day for all that uncomplicated fun. Some were already splashing in the shallows of the beach area, and Jen stood for a moment, watching the children who were so carefree and unaware of anything but their own enjoyment of the moment.

As she moved on, she could hear ducks and geese flapping across to the other side. After a short stroll along the footpath towards the water-sports centre, Jen spotted a bench sheltered by bushes and facing the water. She sat for a moment to gather her thoughts. A small sailing dinghy was out on the lake. It looked like a couple of teenagers sailing. It was perfect for them with its stable buoyancy, small size and 'stitch and glue' construction. Jen remembered doing the same thing in her pre-university days. She smiled at the memory of sailing with her dad, too, and being tipped into the water on more than one occasion when he'd sailed too close to the wind. It had been exhilarating, though. She closed her eyes. A blackbird was singing somewhere not too far away.

She took a deep breath and walked as composedly as she could towards the seat on the far side of the lake. As she had planned, it was not busy over there.

With every step, her heart was pounding. Questions raced through her mind. What should she say? What should she do? How would Mike react? What if he didn't even come?

She had to calm down. This was Mike. They had been together for years before all this trouble had collapsed her world. As Jen passed the thick bushes growing at the edge of the lake, the bench disappeared from view for a few moments. Then suddenly she saw it again, and he was there, not sitting, but standing. She could see his rangy figure walking back and forth. From this distance, she couldn't see the detail of his dark hair, just longer than was fashionable, but she could see its outline. Nor could she see, of course, the crinkles at the corners of his sparkling eyes that she had found so attractive. She thought he was as nervous as she was, though. He put his hand to the back of his neck as he paced. This was it, then; the moment to make her decision and tell him which way she was going.

# CHAPTER 1

## 2005

The end of the summer holidays came quickly that year, as always, but Jen was excited as she drove into the school car park. She had been up early and was ready in good time, anticipating her first day at this new job with exhilaration and nervousness. She'd had to hand in her notice at her previous school by the last day of May. Now September, it had been a long time to wait to take up her post, and she was eager to get started.

There were a few cars there already, but the children wouldn't be back until the following day. During the holidays, when Mike was at work, Jen had been preparing for several weeks now — labelling books and making drawer nametags for her new class. There was some lesson preparation too, of course, but most of that would be done during this afternoon with her partner teacher, Sally Harrison. Sally had been teaching for about the same length of time as herself. Although they had spoken on the phone, they hadn't yet met properly.

Jen climbed out of her car, having made sure not to park right outside the front door in what might be someone else's space. She didn't want to upset anyone on her first day. She looked up and noted the day was cloudy, but the rain seemed to be holding off, which was an optimistic sign. Lifting a bag and a large box from the boot, she staggered towards the main entrance and bent to put the box down to open the door. Someone got to it before her, so she straightened and lurched through.

"Thanks, this is really heavy," she said.

"Here, let me help you with that."

Jenny looked up properly to see a very personable man holding the door for her. He seemed to have a twinkle in his eye and a dimple in his cheek as he smiled at her.

"If you are the new teacher, I understand Charlie will be with you this year," he said.

"I do have a Charlie Mayhew. I've been writing names on books and planning various bits, so I am getting to know names. Would that be him?"

"Yes. I'm his dad. My name's Christopher." His shirt sleeves were rolled up as he held out strong, browned arms and capable-looking hands. He nodded at her in lieu of shaking hands, since his were now full of her heavy box.

Jen noted the flash of smile again and liked him.

The deputy headteacher, Sheila, appeared and sailed towards them. "We meet again. It's lovely to have you here, and I hope you'll settle in happily."

"I'm sure I shall."

"I see you already have a helper. Hello, Christopher," Sheila said in a jolly voice.

"I was just leaving. I came to collect the term dates. I seem to have lost my copy, but I'm being a Good Samaritan now." He smiled.

Sheila carried on. "Sorry we can't have teachers in when the caretaker's not in. I know in some schools you can do that, but it's because of the central alarm system here. Jim, the caretaker, took his holiday late this year. Anyway, I'm sure you'll catch up. The teaching assistants are really good and often stay on a bit to help out. Shall I show you the way?" She breezed off without giving Jen time to reply.

Jen and Christopher exchanged a furtive glance and a conspiratorial smirk as they followed Sheila down the corridor. When they arrived in her new classroom, Jen's tummy did a flip. This was the feeling she had tried to explain to Mike this morning, but she knew he didn't really get it. It smelled like all classrooms seemed to — a mixture of cleaning fluid, polish and something else that was unique to schools — not unpleasant, just familiar. She took in the arrangement of tables and straight away started thinking what she needed to move. She wanted to make it hers somehow.

Christopher put the box on a table and Jen suddenly remembered he was there.

"Thanks so much."

She was rewarded with a sunny grin.

"No problem," he said as he left.

"We'll all be meeting in the staffroom in about half an hour," Sheila said. "Will you find your way back alright? Nearly opposite the front door."

"Yes, that's fine and thanks," Jen said.

"Sally will be next door at any moment," added Sheila. "I'm sure she'll re-introduce herself when she arrives, and you'll be able to come down with her."

Jen thought that would be a good idea. She didn't totally relish the thought of entering the staffroom for the first time alone.

"Well, I'll leave you to it and see you soon." A smile appeared on Sheila's broad face as she left.

As Jen surveyed her space, she secretly hugged herself with happiness. She immediately started sliding tables around into groups that suited her teaching style and would benefit the pupils. She didn't hear another person come into the room and jumped as she turned to pull another table.

"Hi," said Sally jauntily. "Here we are again. It doesn't seem long since I was pulling backing paper off the walls with the teaching assistants and tidying away for the holidays. I'm Sally, by the way. It seems a while since we spoke on the telephone. We're to be partners in crime, so to speak."

"Jen," Jen answered as she stuck out her hand. It was a slightly awkward moment, but Jen knew she would be friends with this young woman with the bouncy ponytail and cheerful voice.

"I'm glad it was you who got the job. I like it here a lot, but they're all older than me and it'll be good to be working with you," Sally said. "I see you've started to get settled in. It's always good to make the room feel like your own. I'll pop back in about twenty minutes, and we'll go to the staffroom together if you like."

"That would be perfect." Jen breathed a sigh of relief.

As they walked up the corridor shortly after, Sally chattered inconsequentially, which enabled Jen to take stock of her surroundings. Some of last term's work was left on the boards to make it feel welcoming for this new school year. The colours were cheerful, and the work was delightful and well-presented. Jen had made a good move, coming here.

On their way, Jen and Sally passed the caretaker, who grinned and said, "Hi ladies, no glitter this term, *please*, especially nearer to Christmas."

"Hello, Jim. We've planned it for next week," said Sally with a light laugh. "This is Jen Lucas. She'll be using it too, so there'll be twice as much to hoover up."

"Pleased to meet you, Jen."

"And you, Jim. I promise to be good. I know that *grime* doesn't pay."

"The old ones are the best ones." He smiled at her slightly feeble joke and she grinned back, feeling more relaxed.

As they entered the staffroom, Jen could see that several people were there before them. Two or three were getting tea and coffee organised for everyone, and some were already seated. She and Sally took two chairs by the windows and Sheila asked them what they'd like to drink. Sally explained that all the staff joined in equally in most things like this, which made for an easy-going atmosphere.

"How's your mum, Sally?" asked one teacher from a seat at the end.

"She's much the same, I suppose," replied Sally. "Although she's in the wheelchair most of the day now. I'm so grateful to Age Concern. While I'm here, someone comes in to clean now and they're organising transport for her to keep her appointments. I'm worried about her being on her own most of the day, though."

"Well, I'm glad I don't have to cope with all that," said the teacher.

Jen was a little surprised that someone would voice their opinion so bluntly, although it sounded like Sally did have a lot on her plate. However, she seemed to be a very sunny, cheery person.

Sally introduced the teacher who had asked after her mum. She was Lesley, a Year 4 teacher. Her teaching partner was Mary. They were sitting next to each other, and clearly got on well as they resumed their whispered conversation. Just as Jen was being informally introduced to several others, the door opened and Graham Lockwood, the headteacher, arrived for the staff meeting. He welcomed Jen and the session started.

# CHAPTER 2

A couple of weeks later, Jen already felt very settled at Holly Road School. The class of six-year-olds were delightful. She enjoyed the stimulation of lesson-planning with another teacher, and the routines of the staffroom and playground were generally enjoyable too.

It was nearly six o'clock on the Friday of her third week when she arrived home. Time had flown by after school as she'd marked the last few maths books, and pasted and trimmed some children's work onto backing paper and planned how she was going to arrange it. Teaching assistants helped, but Jen loved every minute of it. It was the type of school that was buzzing with enthusiasm and while she was tired at this end of the week, she was exhilarated too.

"Hi, I'm home," she called as she took her key out of the front door and pushed it shut with her foot. Her hands were full with yet another box of books and bits, and a bag of tools — a paper trimmer, a stapler, and glue — was swinging from her arm.

Jen knew Mike was already home; she'd seen his car parked outside.

"I'm in the bedroom," came the reply.

Jen dumped her stuff in the corner of the living room and went upstairs to say hello to her husband.

On entering the bedroom, she gave him a quick kiss as he stood by the window, looking out at the small garden below. Then she plonked down onto the bed.

"Phew, I'm whacked," she said, "but I've had a great day. You'll never guess what Sian Day said just before break this morning. She was nearly crying, and when I asked her what was wrong, she said, 'I don't want to be a teacher when I grow up anymore.' When I asked her why not, she said, 'I don't want eyes in the back of my head, and Mum says you must have eyes in the back of your head to know what we're up to all the time.' I nearly laughed but didn't. I managed to cheer her up and showed her that my head was normal."

There was little response from Mike, just a half-hearted smile.

"How was your day?" Jen asked, perhaps a little too brightly.

"Okay, I suppose," Mike answered, not turning. "You're late again."

Jen didn't like the sound of that statement. "Well, you know what it's like — difficult to get away sometimes, so much to do."

"Yes, I know that by now. Anyway, what's up this evening, anything?" he asked, turning to edge around the bed.

"Nothing much," she replied. "I've got some work to do at some point." She cringed inwardly. "But I don't need to do it tonight. I could leave it until tomorrow or Sunday morning. What about going down the road for a drink later?"

"I'm just tired," he said. "What's for tea?"

"I've no idea at the moment, but I'll go and look." She was tempted to ask if he'd bothered looking, but she decided, yet again, to be conciliatory as she left the room.

Mike was not enjoying his work, as she was. He was a manager at a major insurance broker in town. It was a large office and he had to deal with commercial and personal lines, but if he wasn't sorting out problems created by his staff, he felt he was chasing problems for clients. That was how he described it, anyway. Jen tried hard to understand what he did on a daily basis, and it did sound irksome sometimes.

However, he always wanted to be the best, and it seemed to her that he put too much pressure on himself. He had a big presentation evening coming up, when he would need to show his technical knowledge of products on offer, but Jen thought that sounded like an exciting thing to be undertaking.

"How's the planning going for your presentation evening?" Jen asked, genuinely interested, when he appeared in the kitchen.

Mike exhaled. "Oh, I suppose it's okay. Let's not talk about work now, though. It's Friday, for goodness' sake."

"Shall we have a glass of wine, while I sort tea?" she asked, biting her tongue.

"I think I'll go to the gym," Mike said and turned to go back upstairs. "I'm going to get my stuff."

"Right," said Jen. "Are you eating when you get home, then? Only I'm starving already."

"I'll get something myself, later," he called back over his shoulder.

"See you in a bit, then," she said as he disappeared. "Right." Jen sighed in the direction of the door, which was already closed.

Three hours later, she heard the front door open again as Mike arrived home. In his hands he held a bunch of flowers that he had clearly bought in the all-night supermarket. Jen didn't mind that. She was touched that he had bought them for her and guessed that they were meant as an apology.

"They're lovely," she said. "Thank you." She kissed him lightly. No more was said about the tensions of earlier. Jen acknowledged that this was Mike's awkward way of making amends for his surly attitude.

September turned into October, and already there were signs of autumn. Jen needed a coat now, especially for playground duty. This particular morning the low sky made her miss the carefree days of summer. In the front garden the pale pink fuchsias bobbed in the breeze like teardrops as she hurried up the path to her car. She didn't think they would last much longer. A few fallen leaves whirled by the gate. As she arrived at school and parked, the first drops of rain were starting to beat against her windscreen. Jen hoped it didn't presage a bad day. It was Thursday, and Jen usually liked Thursdays. She had a parent helper who came into her class, and an extra pair of hands and eyes was always welcome.

Hurrying indoors, she passed the staffroom. She recognised the hushed voices of Lesley and Mary and the clatter of plates and cutlery as they presumably emptied the dishwasher. Jen had no desire to join that duo.

She had done much of the classroom preparation before leaving the previous evening. Now, she just had some books to take out of her bag, ready for the group of children who would be working with Sian Day's mum. As she switched on her laptop and started loading the programme for the interactive whiteboard, her door opened and Sheila popped her head round. She looked uncharacteristically grim and serious.

"Christopher Mayhew, Charlie's dad, is here to see you. You can use my room. Might be best." She came further into the room and hurriedly whispered, "Charlie's had an accident. I don't know the details. Christopher seems quite distressed. He asked specifically for you."

Charlie Mayhew was a delightful little boy with a round face, bright green eyes, and very curly hair. He was quite small for his age but could stand up for himself when required. Jen was very fond of all the children in her care, but the fact that

Charlie's mum had died when he was only three years old ensured that she had a special regard for him and his courageous cheerfulness. She had reflected, when they met, that he probably only had hazy memories of his mum, but a week after Jen had taken over the class he had brought a photograph of her for 'show and tell'. Jen's heart had flipped. She remembered how she had caught her breath, plumbed the depths of her sensitivity and smilingly achieved the best tone of normality, trying to make the right noises for both Charlie and the other children.

Hastening back up the corridor now, Jen greeted Christopher Mayhew. As she shook his hand, she placed her other hand under his elbow in a gesture of warmth.

"Come this way," she said as she led the way into Sheila's small office next door to the staffroom.

"It's Charlie," he said before she had closed the door. "He was knocked off his bike yesterday after school."

Jen inhaled sharply and said, "Tell me what happened." She indicated the chairs and they sat opposite each other, Charlie's dad on the edge of his.

"He's in hospital. He's got to stay for a while. I've come from there now, but I have to get back."

It explained the shadows under his green eyes and the pallor of his skin.

"He was on his bike, and he rode out in front of a delivery van. He skidded, fell off and hit his head on the kerb. There was so much blood. I shouldn't have let him ride out like that. It's all my fault. I shouldn't have let him out, but all the children ride their bikes up and down the Close." Mr Mayhew rubbed his face with the heels of both hands, and Jen could see he was exhausted and close to tears. He hadn't had time to shave and his wavy, dark hair was tousled. "He's fractured his skull. It's all my fault," he repeated.

Jen was nearly moved to tears too, but she held herself together and said, "Mr. Mayhew, Christopher, you had to let him out to play with the others at his age, and your Close must be safer than many places."

"I kept looking out of the window while I was getting things together for his tea. No-one normally comes down at that time of day. I always make sure he's in before people come home from work, and I finish my work early so I can come and get him from school and give him attention. He had his helmet on when I last looked out of the window, so I don't know what happened there. There was nothing wrong with the strap. He must have taken it off."

"I know you look after Charlie really well," said Jen reassuringly. "What have the doctors said?"

"Well, I called the ambulance because of the blood. Then on the way to the hospital he started vomiting such a lot, and they're keeping him in. I've stayed overnight with him. He's had X-rays, of course, and a CAT scan last night. They put some dye into him, and I had to say if he was allergic to shellfish but I didn't know. At his age he won't eat anything like that. They asked so many more questions as well. They've put in a line to drain some pressure. He was asleep, so the nurse said I should come home and get some things."

Just then, the door opened and Sheila spoke urgently. "Christopher, they want you back as soon as possible. The hospital just rang. They couldn't get through to you and they said it was urgent."

"Oh, my Lord! I have to go." Christopher shot up out of his chair. "Sorry," he said.

"Let us know what…" Jen began, but the door closed before she could finish. As she watched through the glass panels, Christopher turned and gave her a quick wave before running on towards his car.

" This seems so unfair with everything else he's had to cope with," Sheila said. "Are you okay?" Sheila had noticed Jen's tight expression.

"Yes, oh, yes, I'm fine," Jen said, although she felt shaken.

Charlie was such a lovely little boy. She desperately hoped he would be alright.

The previous week, at her first parents' evening in this school, Jen had discovered that Christopher Mayhew was a financial adviser who largely worked from home. She knew he managed his appointments and subsequent paperwork to fit in with Charlie's schooling. He took his role as a single parent very seriously, and tried hard to be father, mother and everything else to Charlie. It must have been very difficult indeed, managing his grief when his wife had died of cancer while coping with the feelings of his young son, never mind all the day-to-day work and responsibilities that he had. Charlie seemed happy and from what he'd told her at school, Christopher always seemed to find the time to take him swimming or to visit his grandparents at the weekends.

As she slowly walked back towards her classroom, Jen called in next door to tell Sally what had happened. Sally was as shocked as Jen was.

"Oh, no! That's dreadful. Poor man. He does so much and copes so well. I really admire him. I've always thought we have so much in common, him and me. I have to look after Mum and he has to look after Charlie, both of us on our own. It's hard to get out and meet other people. Oh, this is awful."

Jen told her the details and assured Sally she would let her know when she knew more.

The day wore on in much the usual way, but Jen felt a heaviness that was hard to disguise and, unusually, she was glad when the time came for the children to leave at the end of the school day.

Before she left for home, there was a telephone call for her. One of the cleaners came to tell her and she rushed along the corridor to the office. Christopher was at the other end of the line. The sound was echoing and hollow, and Jen guessed he was using his mobile phone, perhaps from the foyer of the hospital.

"How is he?" she asked, dreading the answer in case the news was bad.

"He's had an operation. The doctor had to take away part of his skull and remove a blood clot."

There was a strange, stifled sound and then a long pause.

"Christopher, are you okay? Is Charlie alright?"

"Sorry," he continued after several seconds. "The clot was pushing his brain, but they say he'll be alright. I don't know."

"Is anyone with you, Christopher, to help and support?" Jen asked, because she could hear the distress in his voice.

"Yes, well, Mum's on her way," he answered.

"Christopher, it sounds positive. Believe that," Jen said, and then after a pause she added, "Thank you *so* much for letting me know."

"I have to go now. I don't want to be away from his bed."

"Of course. If there's anything you need or I can help with, *please* do let me know straight away."

"Thanks, Mrs Lucas. Bye."

The phone went dead, and Jen sank onto the secretary's empty chair. She sat for several moments, willing everything to be alright before heaving herself up. She called into Sally's room to relay the latest news. Sheila and Mr Lockwood, the headteacher, had left for the day. She knew she would also need to tell them the next day.

"I'd really like to visit after school tomorrow," Jen said to Sally. "Do you think it would be alright to do that? Even if I can't see Charlie, I do feel I'd like to be there to offer some support."

"I'd like to come too," Sally said straight away. "I'm sure it'll be okay. If we can't see Charlie, at least his family will know we're there in case they want anything fetching."

Agreeing to bring her along, Jen headed for home.

# CHAPTER 3

That evening, Jen was home before Mike. She really hoped he would be home soon. She needed to share her day and the distressing thoughts that would not leave her alone. There was some lesson preparation to do; she was finding it difficult to get motivated, but perhaps it would help to settle her. With that thought, she went to get the books out of her bag to take to the table. She had just arranged her things and opened the first book when she heard Mike's key in the front door.

"Hi," he said as he came into the room and gave her a small kiss on the cheek.

"Mike, I'm really glad you're here. I heard about the most awful thing today. One of my children has had an accident and is in hospital with a fractured skull."

"Nasty," he said, frowning. "I've had a crap day too."

"His name is Charlie and his mum died three years ago, so now he's on his own with just his dad."

Mike wandered away into the kitchen and shouted through, "So how long will he be in hospital? One less for you to worry about."

"What?" said Jen. "One less for me to worry about?" She was incredulous as she got up to follow him into the kitchen.

"Well, you're always saying your class is too big. One less, for a while."

"Mike, I can't believe you just said that. He's got a fractured skull. They've taken some of his skull away to remove a big blood clot. It's awful. And I'm not *always* saying my class is too big."

"Sorry." Mike looked sheepish. "I've had a dreadful day. Colin in the office has completely messed up with one of our big clients. This guy has a massive account through us and he's fuming. I've had him shouting in my ear down the phone on and off all day. I think I've begun to pacify him now, but I've got to talk to Colin tomorrow … again. It's not the first time."

"I'm sorry you've had a rough time," Jen said, disappointed.

Perhaps she had timed her news badly. Was she being too involved with a pupil and his circumstances? She had a few moments of reflection while Mike made himself a cup of tea. No. She really didn't think so. This wasn't some angry hiccup over money. This was life and death. She had one more try.

"Mike, this child is seriously ill, and his family circumstances are already dreadful." She wanted and needed some sympathy and understanding. She had tried hard to be diplomatic recently. She understood that Mike's work was draining, but her work was important too. She lifted her chin and said, "I shall be a bit late tomorrow. I'm going to the hospital to visit."

"That's a bit above and beyond, isn't it?"

"No, it's not. It's what any teacher would do in the circumstances." She turned away.

"Well, I know you get paid more than me, but it doesn't mean you have to live and breathe the flaming job," he said.

This was sounding suspiciously like an argument brewing, and Jen slid away from that whenever she could with Mike. She was far more confident in other aspects of her life. She could deal with difficult colleagues and challenging parents far better than with her own husband. She had never even considered that she earned more than him. Their money went into one shared pot, so why was he bringing it up now?

"I've already said I'll go with Sally tomorrow, but I'll try not to be too late," she said in a conciliatory voice, although she felt resentful of Mike's attitude.

"I told Doug I'd be at the gym this evening by six-thirty," Mike announced. "I could do with a good workout to get this day out of my system. I'll get something to eat after, so don't wait."

With that, he poured the rest of his tea away, went to collect his bag from the wardrobe upstairs and left, banging the front door behind him.

The next day, as soon as was decently possible after the children had left in the afternoon, Jen gathered her bags together and went to get Sally.

"I'm off to the hospital," she said. "Do you still want to come?"

"Yes, absolutely. I've just got to put this away, and then I'll be there. I'll see you at the front door in two minutes."

Jen waited until Sally arrived.

"Are you sure you don't mind driving?" Sally asked. "I'm not keen unless I know exactly where I'm going, and it's at the other hospital that Mum usually has her appointments."

"No problem," said Jen as they walked towards her car. "I love driving. Just sling your stuff in here with mine." She opened the boot. As they pulled away, Jen asked after Sally's mum.

"She needs a lot more care these days. It's arthritis, so she can do less and less. I get her up in the morning and get her sorted and into her wheelchair. We've had some alterations done to the house so she can get about, and we've got grab handles everywhere so she can use the bathroom and so on. I do worry, though. If she had a fall, she's got a mobile phone and one of those BT panic button things, but she'd still have to wait. If she hurt herself…" She trailed off. "She's on her own a lot."

"It sounds really tricky for you, trying to balance everything." Jen was sympathetic.

"Everyone who has a job has their own balancing act," Sally said.

"That's certainly true to an extent. Since we're on the subject, you don't think this visit is over the top in terms of taking an interest in what happens to a pupil out of school, do you?"

"Certainly not," said Sally. "Why do you ask that?"

"Well, Mike and I sort of had words about it last night."

"There you are, you see — the balancing act."

Reassured, Jen smiled. "Well, that's how I saw it, and then I had a crisis of confidence."

"Christopher Mayhew is a wonder of a modern man." Sally grinned. "He has such a lot to balance, but he seems to manage amazingly well. And here's us worrying about what we have to do."

"Absolutely," said Jen, feeling relieved and now completely justified.

Having arrived at the hospital, they crossed the shiny floor to the reception desk to ask where to go. Then they took the lift to the paediatric intensive care unit and pressed the buzzer at the security door. The nurse who came to answer their request went and returned after a minute to say that she had consulted with Charlie's father, who had said it was fine for them to visit. They both used the hand sanitiserat the door and entered.

There were eight beds in the ward, but only two were occupied. Jen saw Charlie straight away. Christopher was at his bedside, looking extremely tired. When he saw them, he came straight over. Charlie was sleeping and so he was able to have a quiet word. Again he explained that the doctors had removed part of his skull to take out the blood clot.

"It'd depressed his brain by about two centimetres," he told them.

Jen was horrified, and it must have shown on her face.

"Things are much better now, though," Christopher added quickly. "He's most likely going to be fine, and they say he will probably move to a more normal ward very soon."

"Oh, that's such a relief," said Jen.

Sally added, "I can't imagine what you have been through, but that's such good news."

"They've fitted his skull back together with a titanium plate, apparently," Christopher said. "He's sleeping at the moment, but do go and see him. I'll wait over here because they don't want more than two people at a time, although it's quite quiet in here at the moment."

Jen and Sally moved to Charlie's bedside.

"Poor little mite," Sally whispered.

Jen touched his forehead and gently smoothed the little bit of hair she could see poking under the gauzy bandages that were wound around his head. There were a lot of tubes and pieces of equipment, which all seemed quite scary when neither of them knew what each machine was for, but the care he was receiving was clearly amazing. Charlie stirred in his sleep and the corner of his mouth almost smiled.

Sally left the bedside to move across to where Christopher was watching them. She touched his arm and Jen could see from the expressions on their faces that she was reassuring him.

Jen stayed watching Charlie's little sleeping form, taking comfort from the news that Christopher had told them when they'd arrived.

"We better go," she whispered as he came towards her. "We don't want to stay long and get in the way."

Jen knew Christopher needed to be with his son, but she was glad they'd gone. As they said their goodbyes, Sally led the way towards the door beyond the nurses' station.

Christopher gently caught Jen's arm and said, "Mrs Lucas, thank you for coming. It means a lot to both of us. My mother's just popped back to my house to collect a few items, but I'm sure she'd want me to express her gratitude too.."

"Please, it's Jen, and really I'm not doing anything special at all. I can't help but be involved. It all sounds a little more positive today. Let me know what happens, won't you?"

"I will. They'll do another scan in the morning and we'll know more then."

They said their goodbyes.

"I'm really glad we came," said Jen to Sally, who clearly agreed with her.

# CHAPTER 4

A few days later, Jen was home from school comparatively early when there was a knock at the door. When she answered it, Pat was standing wrapped in her coat, shivering slightly in the fresh autumn breeze.

"Hi!" she said. "Is this a convenient time for a chinwag? I've just dropped the boys at the leisure centre with Doug. He's giving them a swimming session."

"Any time is a convenient time for a chinwag." Jen laughed. "Come on in, and I'll put the kettle on. We've got at least an hour before Mike gets home. It seems ages since we've had a good natter."

"That's what I was thinking," said Pat. "I wanted to hear all about how the job is going. There's something I need to sound you out about too," she added mysteriously.

They went into the kitchen, where Jen made coffee for them both. Where Pat had a table, Jen had a large chest freezer, which was ideal for monthly shopping when she was busy with work. Unlike Pat's homely space, Jen's kitchen was purely functional. She and Pat went into the living room and each settled down on the sofa.

"It's getting quite chilly out there now. Summer's well and truly gone. So, you've been at this school for several weeks now. How's it going?" asked Pat.

Jen told her about Charlie's accident. The last time she had spoken to Christopher Mayhew, however, the news had been much more positive. Charlie had been moved to the usual children's ward and Christopher was hoping he would be home soon. Charlie's grandmother and he had been taking it in turns to stay at the hospital, although Christopher had told Jen that she'd had to leave for her own home again.

"This Christopher certainly has a job and a half," Pat said sympathetically. "I bet he's glad for any help he can get."

Jen was reluctant to tell Pat about her disagreement with Mike over her visit to the hospital. It seemed disloyal, somehow, but in the end it was Pat who brought it up.

"I gather from Doug that Mike was not too pleased about you visiting."

"Oh, so they've been gossiping, have they?" Jen was disgruntled. So much for loyalty. With that, she proceeded to tell Pat everything.

Pat then added vociferously, "I think it was absolutely appropriate. Okay, it's not within the job description, but it's compassionate. Where would we be without a bit of generosity?"

Jen was mildly surprised at the vehemence that Pat was showing on her behalf. She also noticed how tired Pat looked. She had grey smudges beneath her eyes and her short bobbed hair looked tousled.

"Anyway, how is the rest of school going? Are you enjoying it there?"

"Most of the staff are really great. They're friendly, hardworking, and supportive. But there are a couple of teachers who seem to like to mutter in the corner," Jen said. "They don't really affect me too much."

"I bet I know who one of them is," Pat said. Her children were at the school, so she had a good idea of the politics of the place.

"The headteacher seems to know his stuff. He's quite high profile around the school, which is good, but he larks with the children too, so they like him. Mind you, he can have a good voice on him, if they mess him around."

"Yes, I like him. He's turned the place around since he's been there."

"He did an excellent assembly the other day." Jen launched into the detail enthusiastically. "He asked for a volunteer to come and try something really tasty and to guess what it was. Well, you can guarantee one of the Year 6 boys will always go for it. He blindfolded the lad. Then he produced two tins, one was dog food and one was chocolate custard. He took the dog food tin and gave the boy a spoonful of it."

At this point Pat's expression was incredulous and somewhat horrified.

"You can imagine the reaction of the children," Jen continued. "Of course, really, the boy tasted the custard. The Head had swapped the labels over. He made a lot of it, asking the boy if he was enjoying it and would he like some more and so on. Eventually he told the school what he had done and what was really happening. The whole point being that you can't tell from the outside what the inside is really like — just like people. Great! The whole school had been in a bit of an uproar, but he got them back on side in the blink of an eye. Such skill."

"I imagine the children will remember that point for a long time," Pat said. "You were much more animated telling me about all that. I can see you're really enjoying the work."

"Yes, I really am," said Jen.

"Don't worry about a little row. It happens."

"Mmm. What about you? Is there anything wrong, Pat? What did you want to sound me out about?"

It was unusual for Pat to pop round on a weekday during term time. She looked down, avoiding Jen's concerned gaze.

"Pat? If you'd rather not say, that's fine, of course, but it's not like you to be so down."

Tears came to Pat's eyes, and she rummaged up her sleeve for a tissue. "I think, well, I'm sure really, that Doug's up to his old tricks again. He's doing a lot of long shifts and seems so distant and ... I don't know, shifty. The other day, I came back from the shop round the corner and he rang off the phone really abruptly with the old chestnut of a wrong number. He *never* leaves his mobile lying around now, and he *always* used to. I know these signs."

Jen had heard from Pat that Doug had had an affair shortly after their first son was born. She had discussed it at length with Jen and come to the conclusion that he just hadn't been ready to be a new dad. The reality had not been what he'd been expecting and he'd realised, too late, that babies take up an inordinate amount of time. Pat had blamed herself too. She'd said that perhaps she'd devoted too much time to the new child and not enough to Doug. Perhaps she hadn't paid enough attention to her looks and figure following the birth. Jen privately wondered about this last point, however. She gathered that money had been tight, and Pat had been incredibly tired with a baby who didn't sleep at night and cried for much of the day. Jen understood some of the fall-out that Pat still suffered to this day. She was inclined to blame herself for every small thing that went wrong, and she certainly went out of her way to keep Doug happy.

Jen had liked Doug, but he was very vain. She thought it went with sporting types. "Have you confronted him at all?"

"No, not yet. What do you think I should do? If I don't say anything, perhaps it will just blow over. Maybe I'm being over-imaginative because it happened before. I thought we were getting on so well. During the summer we went out for several days with the boys — down to the lake and so on — and we had some really great times."

"I really don't understand it. Maybe some men need constant reassurance of their appeal, or maybe it's just the fun of the chase. You really need to know if he is seeing someone else, though, don't you?" Jen said. "Or you'll drive yourself round the bend."

"I suppose so." Pat sighed.

"How are things in the bedroom department?" Jen hazarded.

"Definitely not brilliant, but I put that down to him being so busy and tired."

Jen looked at her friend quizzically.

"Okay," said Pat, "I'm being naïve and kidding myself, aren't I? I'm making excuses for what is blatantly obvious to anyone else."

Just then, Jen's mobile rang. "I'll ignore that," she said.

"No, get it," Pat snuffled. "I need to visit the loo, anyway, to do a quick repair job."

As she got up, Jen reached for her phone and saw that it was Diana calling. They were friends, but Jen hadn't spoken to her in what seemed like ages. "Hello, Di."

"Hi. How are you? Haven't seen you in ages. How's the job going?"

Jen really didn't feel like a repeat conversation at this moment. Her mind was on Pat's news. "I'm really enjoying it. It's very full-on."

"I heard you were really busy."

"Oh? Who's been telling tales — out of school, so to speak?" Jen laughed.

"I bumped into Mike at the gym and he was telling me."

"Right, he didn't say."

"Well, it was only a quick conversation. I was really phoning to see if you could use some fabric I've got, in the classroom, or in the school somewhere. There are four lots each of three metres. It's like lining material. Mum was having a clear-out, so I took them."

"That's great," Jen said. "I can certainly put them to good use. Thanks."

"I'll put them in the car and drop them round soon, then, or I'll give them to Doug or Mike to deliver if I bump into either of them again."

"I didn't know you had become a keen keep-fitter," Jen said.

"Well, you know…" answered Diana ambiguously.

Just then, Pat came back into the room, so Jen finished her call.

"There, I'm all mopped up and back on track," Pat said as she came through the door.

Jen smiled at her. Trying to normalise the moment, she said, "That was Diana on the phone. She's got some fabric I can use in school. Her mum gave it to her, and she thought of me, which is really kind of her. She can be thoughtful like that."

"Mmm," said Pat vaguely.

"Do you want another coffee?"

"No, I better get going. They'll all be home soon."

"Are the boys okay?" asked Jen.

"They know nothing, and I'm fairly sure they haven't picked up any vibes. They both seem normal enough."

As Pat put on her coat, Jen said, "Let me know what happens, won't you? I hate to think of you so unhappy."

At that moment, the front door opened and Mike arrived home from work. "Hello," he said.

"Hello and goodbye," replied Pat with her head down. "Just off. See you both soon."

Jen saw her to the front door, giving her arm a friendly squeeze as she left. Pat turned and gave a half smile which didn't quite reach her eyes.

"She seemed eager to be gone," Mike observed.

"Did you know she and Doug are having problems?"

After a moment's hesitation, he answered, "Yes, I did."

"Why didn't you say?"

"He asked me not to."

"Is he seeing someone else?"

"He didn't want me to say, because he thought you'd tell Pat."

"Well, she has a good idea already. Who is it?"

"It's someone who works at the poolside. I don't really know," he said.

*I bet you know a lot more than you're telling me*, thought Jen. "I can't bear to see such a good friend so upset," she said. "How long has it been going on?"

"Look, I really don't know much about it. A few weeks, I suppose."

"Oh, hell's bells." Jen sighed, feeling dreadful for her friend.

It seemed that she'd had nothing but sad, bad news recently.

# CHAPTER 5

On Saturday, Jen did the housework while Mike was at the gym again, and she did her lesson-planning on Sunday morning, as usual. Mike was somewhat surly for most of the weekend. Jen tried hard to be cheerful and chatty but began to wonder if she was making the atmosphere worse, so on Sunday afternoon she sat and read quietly. This was something she did so rarely that she almost felt guilty sitting around. Mike went out into the garden and did some tidying up, vaguely hoeing around the plants and sorting out the shed. Then he came indoors and fixed the wobbly handle on the kitchen drawer.

*Well, at least our row is getting all those jobs done,* Jen thought wryly.

During the evening, they skirted around each other politely.

By Monday morning, Jen was feeling mutinous. She didn't know what she should do to create a better mood at home, and she was not sure whether she had done anything amiss to provoke this atmosphere anyway. The more she considered it, the more certain she was that she'd done nothing wrong in going to the hospital to visit Charlie. Mike's words regarding her earnings had upset her more than she'd realised at the time, and as the afternoon wore on she began to feel increasingly rebellious. By the end of the day, she had decided she would visit the hospital again. She wanted to see how Charlie was and felt certain that Christopher Mayhew deserved a little support.

After school she made a good start on her preparations for the next day's work, then packed up her things and left for the hospital. Sally had an after-school club, so on this occasion she went on her own.

Arriving at the hospital, she made enquiries at the desk for the ward that Charlie was on now. Having gained the information she needed, she headed for the stairs rather than the lift. The exercise would help to calm her racing mind. She strode along the corridor, passing several doors to sluice rooms, wards and offices on one side while large windows on the other side looked over a rather sad internal courtyard, where pebble beds and large yucca plants looked neglected. The anonymities of a large hospital were always a mystery. There was a kind of hush, but muted noises behind doors made her wonder what happiness or pain was concealed. She was passing the cafeteria when, through the long, thin windows, she spotted Christopher sitting with a coffee cup in front of him. It was quiet at this time of day, and he looked forlorn on his own in the large, echoing room. She pushed the door, but he didn't even turn his head to see who was entering.

As she went across to his table, he looked up and saw her approaching. His expression became much more animated as he rose to greet her.

"Let me get you a coffee," he said.

"No, no," she replied. "I'll go."

She headed to the counter, bought herself a welcome cup of tea and returned to join Christopher. "How is Charlie?" she asked. "It seems like good news that he is in the regular children's ward."

"We're waiting to see Dr Power when he does his rounds tomorrow morning, and I'm hoping he'll say Charlie can come home. I shall be very glad to be home, I have to say. Hospital food is quite good, and it means I've been able to spend most of my time on the ward, but it's still been hard, all this." Christopher frowned as he spoke.

"It must have been really tough," said Jen. "Never mind all the worry."

"I shall have to get into the habit of cooking and cleaning again. The house is a bit of a tip, to be honest. It's quite hard trying to keep Charlie entertained with things that he can do without being too boisterous. It's going to be a test, when I get him home, to do the household things as well." He shrugged and smiled to himself.

"Life must be quite tricky at the best of times without all this," Jen acknowledged. "Has your mum gone home, or is she still around?"

"She had to go. When she realised Charlie was out of danger, I could tell she thought she needed to be at her own house, so I told her we'd be fine. She has a part-time job at the Sue Ryder charity shop. It's voluntary, but other people have to do her sessions if she's not there. Dad's quite capable on his own, sorting himself out at home after work, but I told her to go. They're both so great and they help out such a lot, but we'll be okay, I'm sure. It's been a steep learning curve, being on my own and doing everything, but generally we seem to muddle through."

"Better than that, from what I've seen," Jen said, leaning forward as she spoke.

"I need to get back to doing some work, too. It's been such a relief to be able to work from home, but I normally do that when Charlie's at school. The money hasn't been making itself for the last couple of weeks."

*This guy certainly has a bowl full of problems*, Jen thought.

"Enough about me," Christopher said. He seemed embarrassed. "You're really busy too, and I imagine you came to see Charlie. I do appreciate you coming. He'll be really excited to see you. I know it's not been that long, but I do get a lot of 'Mrs Lucas said…' when he's not in school."

Jen gently acknowledged that this was the way of many young children, and they both rose to go and visit the little boy. Christopher rang the buzzer, and when a nurse pushed the ward door he allowed Jen to precede him through it. Having both stopped to use the obligatory hand sanitiser from the dispenser at the door, Christopher led the way to Charlie. The room was quite large, with several beds. The walls were brightly coloured with large murals of cartoon characters. Even the floor had a giant picture in the middle. There were some small child-sized tables with different coloured tops and chairs to match. Several of the beds had soft toys on them. It did still have a faint hospital smell, however.

Charlie's little face beamed the biggest smile as Jen approached. How different this visit was from the last. He was kneeling up, with a tray of cars on the bed in front of him. His head was still wrapped in a gauzy bandage, which now had stickers all around it. Jen handed him the little parcel she had brought and he eagerly tore the paper off. It was a small box of Lego to make a Transformer. They were all the rage with the boys in her class. Christopher was clearly moved to see his son so happy and revitalised.

Jen spent over half an hour playing with Charlie and chatting easily with Christopher. When she glanced at her watch, she was surprised at how the interval had rushed by.

"I better go," she said. "I still have some school work to do at home before tomorrow, and my husband will think I've disappeared." *If he even notices I'm not there*, she thought.

"I'll walk to the door with you. What do you say, Charlie?"

"Bye-bye. I want to come back to school, tomorrow."

"Well, maybe not tomorrow, but soon. Perhaps I'll be able to come and see you again," Jen said.

"Thank you for my present," Charlie added.

"You chose the right thing there," said Christopher. He turned to Charlie. "I'll be back in a minute, lad, and then we'll see if we can put that together, shall we?"

At the door, Jen had an idea that she thought would help them, but she wasn't sure if Christopher would accept. Hesitantly, she suggested, "I'd really like to cook some freezer meals for the two of you. It wouldn't be any extra work, because I'd be doing food for Mike and me. I could just do a bit extra. It might just help to get you through the next few days until you get back into some sort of routine."

As anticipated, Christopher was full of concern. "I really couldn't put you out like that."

"Well, as I say, it wouldn't be any extra work. I really wouldn't offer if it was going to be a lot of trouble. I'd just like to help. What is this life if we can't do a small service for someone when it might be needed?" She smiled. "I understand if you'd rather I didn't. It was just an idea."

"If you really are sure, it would be a massive help. I'd be able to give so much more attention to Charlie. Really, you must only do meals for a day or two, though, just until I get sorted out."

"That's absolutely fine," Jen reassured him. "I'll drop them round the day after tomorrow. You should definitely be home then, by the sounds of it. If there's any change, just leave me a message at school. Will you be okay for tomorrow if you go home then?"

"I'm sure I can find sausage, chips and beans or something. Thank you again, *so* much."

"I'll see you then. Bye."

Jen left, feeling she was doing something useful. As she walked down the corridor, she turned to see Christopher Mayhew watching her go. She smiled and gave a small wave.

On the way home, Jen hurried into the local supermarket. It was as busy as ever. She rushed around, dodging the trolleys and the staff members re-stacking the shelves, buying things that she could use. She tried to think of nourishing things that she thought a little boy would eat. She bought chicken to make nuggets, and fish to make fingers and minced beef for some meatballs. She added several other ingredients: eggs, bread for crumbs and semolina to make a coating. Having decided she had enough to supplement what she could find at home, she queued up at the checkout.

She waited restlessly, aware that time was creeping onwards quickly and the queue in front seemed to be creeping only slowly. When she finally got to the checkout the till girl was bright and breezy and Jen responded in like manner, although a moment before she had been feeling tense and rushed. She decided the lass must really enjoy her job too and was silently grateful to her, before she hurried home.

When Jen arrived home, she hauled her school bags and shopping into the house, feeling mildly surprised that she had beaten Mike home.

She got straight on with her task and had done the basic preparation for the nuggets and fish fingers by the time Mike arrived.

"I'm in the kitchen," she called. "You've had a long day. Do you fancy a glass of wine?"

"Mm, yes," he answered, sounding vague. "I'll get one in a bit. I just need to shower first, I think. You look busy. What are you doing?" He frowned.

"I'm making a few freezer meals," Jen answered ambiguously. She suddenly wondered what Mike's reaction was going to be.

"Shan't be long, and then I'll get those drinks," he shouted from the bathroom.

As he returned, having showered and changed, Jen was just frying up the chicken nuggets.

"That's a lot for two," Mike observed.

"I'm doing a few extra for Christopher Mayhew and Charlie." Jen winced internally. "I went to the hospital to see how Charlie was getting on, and Christopher said he was hoping they would be able to go home tomorrow."

"So why are you cooking for them, then?" Mike asked quietly.

"Look, Mike," she started in defence. "He's on his own, trying to hold down a job and care for a sick little boy because his wife *died*. It's just a small neighbourly service."

"That's all, is it? And who's paying for all this extra food — you on your mighty big salary, or me on my lowly one?"

*Oh Lord, here we go*, thought Jen, but she was determined to put her point of view across calmly and openly this time. "Mine, if you like," she said. "But I'm sure he'll pay me back. Anyway, as I said, it's just a neighbourly thing to do."

"And what else are you doing for him, to be neighbourly?"

"What's that supposed to mean?"

"Well, since he's on his own, maybe there's something else he'd like you to do for him, or with him."

"Mike!" Jen was horrified. "There's nothing going on, nor would I like there to be. How can you doubt me in that way?" She turned off the gas under the pan and immediately tried to put her arms around him. He turned from her. "Look at me," she said. "Believe me when I say it's you I love, and I have no desire to be with anyone else."

All she was doing was cooking a bit of food. Why was he making this an issue?

"Okay, fair enough, sorry," Mike conceded. "I still don't see why you're doing this. He's just a kid in your class, for goodness' sake."

"Well, I've decided to help out, just for this week. It doesn't need to affect you. Our tea is here too." She turned and switched the gas back on. "It'll be ready in ten minutes."

"I don't think I'm hungry at the moment," he said.

"Well, what about that glass of wine?" Jen asked, trying to mend fences.

"I don't think so, not if I'm driving."

"What do you mean, if you're driving? Where are you going?" She was puzzled. "You didn't say you were out."

"Well, I don't think I need to ask," said Mike. "I've only just decided, anyway. I think I'll go to the gym, since you're so busy."

"But I've got your tea ready here, too," said Jen.

"I'll have it later, or you can add it to Christopher Mayhew's. That seems appropriate."

"Oh, for goodness' sake!" Jen raised her voice now.

She turned to carry on with her task, and as she did so Mike left the room. Five minutes later, she heard the front door slam.

Later in the evening, since there was still no sign of Mike, Jen decided to telephone Pat. The boys would be in bed and she thought Doug would probably be out, given the current circumstances. Hopefully, there would be the chance for a good talk and some advice to help her decide if she was being too stubborn or not. They had spoken on the telephone since Pat's latest news, and Jen knew that Pat was coping in her own way. She'd had practice previously, and she was trying to hold it all together for the children. Pat still hadn't tackled Doug to find out for definite if he was seeing someone else. It was almost as if hiding her head in the sand was less hurtful than knowing the worst.

The phone rang several times before a breathless Pat finally picked up.

"Hello," Jen heard her puff.

"Hi, Pat, it's Jen. Have I called at a bad time?"

"No, no, not at all. I was just upstairs tucking in the boys, and I'd left my mobile in the kitchen. They're all snug now. I love them lots, but this is the best moment of the day, when they're tucked up and I can put my feet up."

Without any further preamble, Jen said, "I think I need some advice." Then, feeling she had been a bit heartless, she added, "But I can call another time. I'm sure you've earned some peace and quiet."

"It's fine. I'm always ready for a chat. What's up? You sound a bit tense."

"Mike and I have had a good few words, and he's stormed out. It's all because I've cooked a few freezer meals for Christopher and Charlie Mayhew, because I think Charlie's coming out of hospital tomorrow." Jen explained how sorry she felt for Christopher and that she was only trying to be helpful. "Mike completely flipped and suggested I was having some kind of fling, for goodness' sake. I would never do that. I made a vow when we got married, and that means a lot to me. On top of that, he's made comments again about the fact that I earn a bit more than him. That's certainly never mattered to me, and I didn't think it was important to him either. We just have a shared account."

"When did that side of things seem to start?"

"Definitely when I started this job," answered Jen. "But he knew the salary before I got it, and he was all in favour of the move. It's no more than I was getting before. I've always earned a little more than him."

"Sounds like he's feeling unhappy for some reason," Pat said. "Any ideas why?"

"The only thing I can think of is that he's very unhappy at work at the moment. That smacks of childish jealousy to me," Jen said crossly.

"Maybe, but perhaps he's feeling a bit insecure," Pat added.

"What's he got to feel insecure about?"

"Perhaps he feels he's not providing enough for you — not just money, but happiness too — and what with this thing with Christopher, maybe he's lacking a bit of confidence."

"You could be right," said Jen, feeling slightly mollified and less irritable.

"Try giving him a bit more time."

"I do try to listen to his troubles, but I suppose I have been a bit wrapped up in work recently. It's all so new and good fun."

"That sounds like part of the trouble to me," Pat observed. "It's all going so well for you; he probably is a bit jealous. That's only human nature."

"You're always so wise, Pat."

"Not in my own life, though," she said. "I'm as sure as I can be that Doug's at it again."

"You still haven't tackled him, then?"

"No, I'm hoping he'll get over it. It's probably me not doing enough to please. I really think he loves us in his own way."

"If you need a friendly ear at *any* time, come round or call, won't you?"

"I will. I'm fine, but thanks anyway. Speak soon. Let me know how it goes."

Jen ended the call and went to have a quick shower. After, wrapped in her dressing gown, she was feeling peckish but couldn't decide whether to eat now or hope that Mike came home soon, so she could make it up to him. She'd had time to think things through, having listened to Pat's advice.

Very soon after, he returned. She hastened to meet him in the hallway and flung her arms around him. Taken a little by surprise, Mike dropped his bag and his arms encircled Jen's waist. He kissed her tenderly and long.

"I hate it when we argue," she whispered.

"Me, too," he responded, taking her hand and leading her to the foot of the stairs.

All thought of food gone, she followed him up. Pushing the bedroom door open, they fell onto the bed and Mike kissed her more forcefully. Jen responded readily, cradling his head in her hand and running her other hand down his cheek, pulling him to her. They gained mutual comfort from their lovemaking, each giving and taking pleasure. There was no giggling, no teasing, no joking. There was an intensity born from their earlier disagreement and a need to confirm, she thought, their relationship. After, she told him again that she loved him and he responded in kind. For now, at least, all was well again.

# CHAPTER 6

A couple of days later, Jen and Mike were still happy. Trust was restored and things were as normal. While they were eating breakfast together, Jen hesitated but eventually said, "Mike, the food I made for Christopher Mayhew…"

"I know," he responded, "you need to take it to him."

"Is that okay? I'm not staying or going in or anything, just delivering."

"Yes, it's fine. I know I was an arse. I trust you, Jen. I know you wouldn't do anything behind my back." He smiled.

His eyes crinkled at the corners and her heart melted all over again. She glanced at her watch, wishing there was time to slip upstairs with him before they both had to leave for work. "I shall ask Sally if she wants to come too," Jen said. "She came to the hospital, that first time. I think she more than likes Christopher."

"If you want to, but don't worry about it anymore," Mike responded.

"I'll see you later, then." Jen stood behind him as he sat and put her arms around him, giving him a quick kiss and nuzzling his ear.

She loaded her plastic containers of meals into a carrier, planning to transfer them into the school freezer to wait until the end of the day. Then she gathered her school bags, ready to leave the house.

"See you tonight. Love you," she called from the door.

There was no response, but she guessed Mike was re-reading something in the paper.

Driving to school, Jen contemplated her situation. She was still slightly uneasy about Mike's recent reactions when she thought hard about it, but really everything seemed to be back to normal. Perhaps she had been too wrapped up in her own work and the needs of others. After all, she and her husband loved each other. They had shared so much together and were good friends as well as lovers.

The school day was pleasant and ordinary. Jen had spoken to Sally at lunchtime, and she was really keen to accompany her to see Christopher and Charlie Mayhew. She had the feeling Sally had been a little put out over the reason for the visit. Since she seemed to like Christopher, maybe she wished she had thought of something practical to do to help out, as Jen had.

In the car, travelling to the house after work, Jen's suspicions were confirmed when Sally said as much. The journey took longer than expected, because at five o'clock the traffic was starting to build up. This gave them the opportunity to exchange a few words.

"I would like to help Christopher more," Sally said. She followed this with a little sigh that spoke volumes. "I admire him and what he does for Charlie. From my experience, I know how difficult and lonely it can be, caring for someone when you're on your own."

"He does a good job," Jen said. "Charlie is a delightful little boy. He's always chatty and confident without being overly so. I hope this incident won't inhibit him in any way."

As they arrived in the correct road, Sally kept an eye on the house numbers as Jen slowly drove. This was the first time either of them had been down this way. It was a cul-de-sac and not very long, so they quickly found where they needed to be. Jen retrieved her cool-bag of food from the boot and Sally opened the gate and preceded her up the path. The front garden was small. There were no flowers, but the small patch of grass was cut and the edges trimmed neatly. Sally knocked and when Christopher came to the door, Jen planned to hand over her bag on the step, enquire after Charlie's health and beat a retreat.

The door opened and Christopher smiled when he saw who it was. Jen moved to hold her bag out and opened her mouth to make a greeting, but Sally almost leaped forwards to explain why they were there.

"Oh, yes, Mrs Lucas, Jen," Christopher said, catching her eye. "You said you'd be bringing me a food parcel." He grinned. "Come in."

"Thank you," said Sally, before Jen could say a word.

"I really can't stay long," Jen added. "Is Charlie up and about?"

"He certainly is," Christopher said. "It's hard keeping him calm enough. He'd love to go out to play, but I think that's a bridge too far at the moment. I'm going to have to be careful not to mollycoddle him, though."

They were shown into a living room in which there were signs of lots of activity. There was a pile of newspapers and magazines under the coffee table, an empty mug on the mantleshelf and a toybox that was full to overflowing in a corner.

"I'm really sorry we're not tidier," said Christopher, casting his eyes around the room and looking sheepish.

"I'm sure you have more important things to do," Jen said. "And anyway, it's much better to see this than an unfriendly place."

"I'll call Charlie. He's up in his room, playing with his cars. Please, sit down." Hastily he removed a computer magazine from one chair and slid a collection of Lego further along the sofa. Jen recognised the Transformer model she had given Charlie and was gratified to know that he had been playing with it.

Just as they sat down, the door flew open and Charlie burst into the room.

Both Jen and Sally were shocked to see him. He had no bandages on now and his hair had been shaved off on one side. His scars were still livid, but he was clearly his normal, exuberant self. Both the teachers said hello, trying hard not to let their feelings show. Jen slid down off the sofa to sit on the floor, taking pieces of the Lego figure in her hand.

"I see you've been making him. Will you show me how he 'transforms'?"

Charlie came and sat down on the floor next to her, and Jen was quite touched when he snuggled in against her to complete the figure. The little boy happily demonstrated his skill to Jen.

While he was occupied, Sally asked Christopher, "What's the next step for Charlie?"

"He has to go to see the doctors as an outpatient next week, Miss Harrison," explained Christopher. "But they seem very pleased so far."

Jen glanced at Sally to see her gaze slide sideways, up to where Christopher was standing.

"Please, call me Sally," she said.

Christopher cleared his throat and there was a pause. Then he spoke again. "We had the nurse call round this morning, and they've given me a leaflet of information — things to look out for and to tell other people, like the school."

"When do you think he might be able to come back?" Sally asked.

"I think I need to come and talk to Mr Lockwood about it. What do you think, Jen? He'll be in your care, and I don't want to be unfair to you by expecting too much."

"I think if you can come into school, the three of us can discuss the things that he'll be able to do or not. We can take it from there."

Charlie continued to play, and the conversation appeared to pass him by.

"At the hospital they indicated that he may be able to come back soon, but perhaps part-time. Do you think that might be an option, Jen?"

"I don't see why not. Ring the office when you're ready, and we'll fix up a meeting," she said.

"I want to come back to school," Charlie joined in.

"I'm sure it won't be too long," Jen said to him. "You want to be able to do things in school without getting too tired, though."

"Is there anything you need?" Sally asked of Christopher. Her eyebrows were raised in question, and she tilted her head to one side as she regarded him, wide-eyed.

"No, we're fine now," Christopher replied, smiling at her, and then he turned to Jen and added, "Thank you so much for what you've done. That's a tremendous help."

"It was really no problem," Jen answered. "I'm afraid I shall need to be going in a minute." She stood to gather her bag and moved towards the door.

"I haven't even offered you a tea or coffee when you have been so thoughtful and helpful," Christopher said, sounding mortified.

"Please, don't even think of it, but I really must be off." Jen turned and spoke to Charlie, whose little round face was looking up at her. "We'll see you soon, won't we?"

He silently nodded, looking tired now. He was probably ready for his tea, bath and bed.

"Ring school when you're ready," Jen repeated as she opened the front door. "See you soon."

As they followed the short front path, both she and Sally waved to Charlie, who was at the window.

Jen dropped Sally off at the school so that she could collect her own car, and then she hurried home. As she pulled up at the kerb outside her house, she could see Mike just going in through the front door.

"Hello," she called out as she went in. "How are you? How was your day?"

"Hi, not bad," Mike answered as he came and gave her a kiss on her cheek. "Mind you, I thought the rollicking I had to give Colin the other week would have woken him up a bit, but I'm still fielding problems he's made. I'm going to set him targets and start some disciplinary stuff if he can't sort himself out." He moved towards the stairs on his way to get changed out of his work suit. "I'm really getting fed up with him."

Jen, having dumped her bags in the corner of the living room, went into the kitchen to start tea. *Oh well*, she thought, *no questions is better than the third degree*. Maybe she would get the chance to share her day later.

# CHAPTER 7

Saturday morning came. Since Mike was out at his usual gym session, Jen had cleaned and put the washing on, so she decided to walk to the paper shop. She needed a bar of chocolate, and she would see if they had the *Times Educational Supplement*. She read it from time to time to keep up with the constant changes and innovations in her work.

It was a chilly but bright late autumn day, so she wrapped up and left the house. It was the sort of weather that was uplifting. Although the wind was blowing, the sun was low and bright and the sky was blue. Bundles of leaves had collected in odd corners where they had been swirled around, but they were dry and crisp.

It wasn't far to the little parade of shops. The newsagent was quite busy and having found her paper, Jen selected a chocolate bar and went to pay. There was quite a queue and just ahead of her she saw Pat. Jen could see instantly that her friend was not well. She looked pale and tired.

"Hello, Pat. I just nipped round for a pick-me-up," said Jen, waving her chocolate.

"I think I need something like that, only times it by ten." Pat smiled, always the optimist. "I'll just pay for this and see you outside, if you've time. We could walk back together."

Jen paid and hurried outside to meet Pat. "Where are the boys?" Jen asked.

"They're away at Mum's for the whole weekend. She came to collect them. She said she wanted to take them to the woods near her for the day because they're having some kind of event there. I didn't argue. They'll all have a great time. Apparently there are all kinds of activities going on and some 'making' thing. Mum's fantastic like that, she'll get stuck right in with them. She just senses when I could do with a break, and I know she enjoys it too. It helps to keep her active now that she's on her own, since Dad died."

"I have to say, you look like you could do with the break," Jen said with concern. "Is there anything I can do?"

"No, no. It's just the ongoing saga of Doug and me. I'm not sure I can take much more, though. I think the boys are taking note of me looking like death warmed up. That's not helping the situation with Doug, of course, either. A bit of a vicious circle, really." She shrugged and sighed.

"Maybe you both need a little time apart for thinking," Jen said tentatively. "Could or would he consider that?"

"I suppose he could go to his mum's, or he's got a good friend at work he might ask. Huh, a male friend, that is." She shrugged. "I think he believes he loves us in his way, but at the moment I feel so useless. I just keep thinking that if he loves us, why does he persist when he *must* know it's hurting us so much? How does he rationalise it all? It must be partly my fault as well, of course, otherwise why would he do it? I feel a total failure, actually. I can't even keep my husband contented. I'm clearly just not enough. After the last time, I told myself we were both too young to have settled. He needed to sow some oats, as they say. I made excuses, I suppose, but perhaps he wishes now he had never got married to me. I just don't satisfy him."

"He must realise you know about his affair, surely? Maybe he's kidding himself that no-one is harmed if it's all covert still, and he can persuade himself that you don't know. Maybe he's reassuring himself that he's still attractive to the opposite sex. I really don't know, but I do think you need to talk," offered Jen.

"I just keep thinking he'll get over it and we can go back to how we were. I can't make him want me. He has to do that for himself."

Jen thought, *It'll never go back to how you were*, but she kept that to herself for the time being. "Yes, but if he's kidding himself that he's not hurting you, he has no reason to leave her alone. I really think you need to talk, or one of you, probably you, is going to be ill, and then what will the boys do?"

"You're right, Jen. I need to say all this to Doug, don't I?"

By this time they had arrived at Jen's house. "Do you want to come in for a cuppa?" she asked.

"I think I'll get home. Strike while the iron is hot and all that," Pat replied. "Since the boys are away, perhaps this is the day to have the discussion with Doug."

"If there's anything I can do, just call me," said Jen. "And let me know how you get on."

"I certainly will, and thanks."

Pat hurried on down the road, and Jen wondered if she would follow through with her new resolve.

As she put her key in the front door, she thought how lucky she was not to be in the position in which Pat had found herself.

Mike was still not home from his Saturday morning session at the gym, although it was 12.30pm. Perhaps he had gone on to do the shopping at the supermarket, as he sometimes did.

However, when Mike came in, he clearly hadn't been shopping. He was in a fine and lively mood, and straight away he put the kettle on for a coffee.

"How was the gym session?" Jen asked.

"Fine," he answered. "I ran 5k on the treadmill and cycled 20k on the bike, so I went for a quick pint in the hotel bar.

Diana was there," he added casually. "She was waiting for Greg to come from work, but he was late."

"How was she? I haven't seen her for ages," said Jen.

"She was okay. She's had her hair cut differently; it looked quite smart."

"Since when did you notice peoples' changes in fashion?" Jen teased, but Mike ignored her comment and finished making the coffee, whistling quietly to himself as he did so.

"We'll have to do the shopping this afternoon," said Jen. "Not very exciting, I know, but needs must."

"Yes, I suppose so. Diana invited us to go for dinner sometime soon. We didn't fix any date, but I said you'd get in touch and sort it."

"That'll be something to look forward to," Jen said.

"She said she'd speak to Pat too," he added.

"I'm not sure what's happening there. I bumped into her at the paper shop this morning and she really didn't look good. Things between her and Doug seem to be going from bad to worse. I suppose you know all about that, though," Jen remarked.

"Well, we'll see then." Mike avoided any more conversation on that point.

"I don't know how I would cope if you were to cheat on me," Jen said wistfully. "You'd tell me, though, wouldn't you, rather than be deceitful?"

"Have an affair?" Mike laughed loudly. "Where did that come from? I expect us to grow old together."

# CHAPTER 8

The weekend had been lazy and non-eventful, but relaxed and enjoyable too. Another Monday morning came all too soon. The morning's teaching went well, with many of the children having good sessions in maths and then English. It was lunchtime before Jen knew it. Time certainly passed quickly here. Feeling buoyant, she took her lunchbox to the staffroom at quarter to one, having prepared her classroom for the afternoon.

Only Mary and Lesley were there before her. This was not unusual. They were having a whispered conversation when she entered, which appeared to stop abruptly. She made herself a drink of hot blackcurrant juice and settled on a seat by the window to eat her lunch. Smiling, she asked if they'd had a good morning, just to make conversation, and she got a brief nod and a grunt that passed for assent. *Oh well*, she thought, *I've made an effort.* Mary turned away from her slightly to ask Lesley a question and Jen felt decidedly cut out of the conversation, so she ate her lunch in silence until the door opened and several others came in.

"Well, you lot are quiet today," announced the deputy headteacher, Sheila. Sally, who had arrived at the same time, smiled and came and sat next to Jen.

Jen stood up to throw her rubbish in the bin. As she did so, her skirt caught on her mug, sending it flying across the carpet and splattering the dregs everywhere.

"Oh, shoot!" she exploded, rushing to the sink for some paper towels and a cloth.

"That'll be there for posterity," said Mary.

"One to remember you by," added Lesley rather meanly as Jen knelt on the floor, alternately dabbing and rubbing.

Although the stain was fading, it was looking distinctly like a permanent fixture.

"I'll bring some special cleaning fluid in tomorrow," Jen said. "I'm really sorry, everyone."

"Never mind, Jen," Sheila consoled her. "Maybe it will encourage Graham to spend the money and change the carpet before too long. It's well overdue."

"Thanks," said Jen. "I'm so sorry, I feel dreadful about it."

"Phew," said one of the others, changing the subject. "I've had a right session with John Daley, so when he said he was going to tell his dad I was being mean, I said I'd welcome the opportunity to tell his dad all about the fact that he hit Stephen Black and used the 'f' word in my maths lesson."

Jen was thankful for a change in the conversation. Mary and Lesley were a right pair sometimes. What had started as quite a good day had turned a little sour.

Just then, the door opened and Graham Lockwood came in. No-one mentioned the stained carpet, but Lesley nudged Mary's arm and Jen could have sworn she smirked as she looked at the stain. Mr Lockwood pinned a new notice on the staffroom board.

"Some of you may be interested in this," he said, and without further discussion he left.

Mary stood to look at the new piece of paper. "Well, well! He's clearly got some money from somewhere, but not for a new carpet."

"Go on, then," Sally said. "Share it out."

"He's advertising for an internal promotion. One extra salary point for some home/school liaison responsibility. I suppose he never did replace Peter's point when he left, and you didn't get it when you came, did you, Jen?" Mary said pointedly.

This lunchtime had been one dig after another.

"What have I done to deserve that?" Jen asked Sally on their way back to the classroom just before the end of the lunch hour.

"Nothing, nothing at all," Sally reassured her. "She's been like that with all of us in turn. You're just the lucky winner at the moment."

"Do you think you'll apply for this point that's on offer?" Jen asked her friend. "You've been here a while, and I'm sure you have the experience."

"It's tempting," Sally replied. "I'll have to think about it, though. It would be more hours after or even before school, and I've got Mum to consider." She sighed.

Jen felt really sorry for Sally at that moment. Just when she could be advancing her career, she had too many other responsibilities holding her back. It must have been very frustrating for her at times, but she put such a brave face on it all. Jen admired her commitment.

As the afternoon disappeared quickly under the weight of a lively technology session using fabric and materials as well as a watering can to find the best material to make a waterproof coat for Talented Ted, the school mascot, playtime arrived in no time at all. Jen was not on duty, and normally she didn't bother to go to the staffroom at this time but stayed in her classroom, making preparations for the last session. This afternoon, however, she was thirsty, since half her drink had ended on the floor. As she entered the room and found it empty, her eye was caught by the head's new notice on the board. At this stage in her career, it would not be unreasonable to consider going for it, but she hadn't been there that long and she didn't know if she would be in with a chance. She decided to discuss it with Mike first, since it meant a few more hours. Then she would go and see Graham Lockwood.

At the end of the day, Jen saw the children out and stood with them until all had been claimed by their parents. As she was waiting with the last two children, Mrs Jones came marching across the playground to her with Johnny in tow.

"I want a word with you," she said forcefully.

*I know what this is going to be about*, thought Jen to herself. "If you'd like to go into the classroom, Mrs Jones, I'll be with you just as soon as these two children have been collected."

As soon as possible, Jen went to speak to Mrs Jones.

"I'm fed up with my Johnny being bullied by Ian Williams," she said.

She continued to shout at Jen for some minutes. Jen knew that Mrs Jones needed to voice it all before it was possible for her to get a word in edgeways. The mother spewed her point of view in a never-ending stream. Eventually, Jen was able to ask Johnny what he thought had happened. Parents frequently came when children had argued. More often than not, it wasn't a case of constant aggression or teasing, which might be genuine bullying, but just a childish scrap. However, such an allegation was to be taken seriously, and Jen knew she would need to talk to both boys in the morning. She promised Mrs Jones that she would act and get back to her after school the next day. Finally, she had calmed down and eventually left in a reasonably pleasant mood. This wasn't the first time Jen had felt the wrath of such a parent, and she knew it wouldn't be the last.

She was packing up her bags when there was a knock on the classroom door. She shouted, "Come in." As she turned to the door, Christopher Mayhew entered.

"I've brought your food boxes back."

"Thank you," said Jen, pleased that this, at least, was a pleasant conversation.

"Are you still okay for Charlie to come in part-time soon?"

Jen, Christopher and Graham Lockwood had had a meeting a few days ago and decided on a protocol for Charlie's re-entry to school.

"Absolutely." Jen nodded. "I'm really looking forward to having him here again."

"I am so grateful to you for all your kindness," Christopher reiterated. "I've just finished reading this."

He produced a paperback from the bag in which he had brought the plastic boxes. "I really enjoyed it. I don't know if it's up your street."

"Thank you," said Jen.

She was aware that Christopher must feel a little indebted to her, and this was probably his way of showing his thanks.

"I've read two of this author's books," she added, "but not this one. I couldn't put the last one down. Do you need it back in a hurry? This one may take me a little longer to read. During term time, I only manage a few pages each night before I drop off to sleep."

He smiled. "No rush."

With that, he thanked her again and left. Jen picked up her bags once more, took her coat from the hook behind the door and followed in Christopher's footsteps towards the front entrance. At least she had a smile on her face now.

Sheila had just come out of her office and was standing at the front door. She was looking out towards the car park. As Jen arrived, she could see what Sheila was watching. Sally was beside Christopher, standing next to his car. She must have been in the car park when he'd emerged from the school.

"I think we have a blossoming romance there," Sheila remarked.

"I think Sally feels they have quite a lot of shared experience," Jen said, smiling. "I'm not sure if Christopher is interested or not though," she added, thinking back to the visit they had both made to Christopher's house recently.

"Well, it's clear she's got the hots for him."

Sally was looking coquettish next to Christopher, laughing and standing close. Sure enough, he edged away slightly, but she reached out and lightly touched his arm, before moving off with what was clearly a smiling goodbye. Jen was unsure what to make of the exchange. She was fairly sure Sally would not say no to a relationship with Christopher Mayhew, but would he reciprocate? She really was not convinced. It would need to be a very strong feeling on his part, Jen thought, to take up with someone when he had, by all accounts, been very happily married and with a such young son. She hoped Sally would not be hurt and disappointed.

Jen arrived home before Mike, and she prepared in her head how she would present the promotion and her point of view. It briefly shot through her mind that she shouldn't need to prepare any kind of argument. If she decided to go for the job, she should do it. However, living with someone else seemed always to require compromise.

Mike arrived home shortly after Jen and, for once, he told her he'd had a good day, landing a major contract that would go down very well when he had his annual one-to-one appraisal. It was Jen's turn to share the events of her day, but on this occasion she refrained, not wanting to put a dampener on the calm atmosphere.

Jen had decided to wait until after tea to have her discussion. After a meal and a glass of wine, they should both be more relaxed.

Once they had eaten, shared some of the day's happenings and cleared away the dishes, Mike headed for the living room and the television. Jen halted him by saying, "Can we have a family conference?"

"That sounds a bit serious," he said.

Jen mentally kicked herself for getting it wrong, especially after all her abstract preparation. Perhaps that was the problem, too much planning on her part. "No, not at all." She laughed. "It's just that an internal promotion has come up at school."

"What does it involve?" asked Mike, naturally enough.

"I don't think it will be too many more hours, because I'm not doing quite as many as when I first started since I know the routines better. It'll also mean a bit more money, of course, and the joint account can always do with that. We could perhaps afford to decorate the living room and buy that larger flatscreen television."

"Hmmm," said Mike. "Well, it's up to you. The money will always come in handy."

"I think I'll talk to Mr Lockwood tomorrow and find out exactly how he sees it going. I'll need to write an application letter and probably go through another interview. I imagine there will be other members of staff who apply."

"Why, who else might want the job?"

"I imagine Sally will. Mary is the only other person who possibly could, I think."

"What, old crabby knickers?" Mike laughed. He had heard her name several times when Jen had told him different things that had gone on in the staffroom.

"Oh, Mike! Yes, the very one, but she has loads of experience at the school. I would have thought she might have got a responsibility point before, but who knows?" Jen replied with a thoughtful frown.

"It sounds like you have decided to apply already, from the way you just said you'd talk to the headteacher about it," Mike observed.

"Well, I possibly will, but I need to talk to him anyway to find out more details. Like I said, I need to ask him how he sees the post being delivered. I'll sleep on it until then. I wanted to see what you thought first, though."

# CHAPTER 9

The next day, Jen decided she would talk to Graham Lockwood. She knocked on his door as soon as she arrived at school.

"Hello, come in," he called.

"Good morning," Jen said. "I wondered if I might have a word about the responsibility point you've advertised on the board."

"Fine, but can we do it after school? I've got a meeting with the finance committee this morning, and I've got some last-minute figures to present to them. It's extra information that's just come in."

"Yes, of course," said Jen, smiling. *Oh, rats, I shall have to control my impatience all day now*, she thought.

After school, while wishing to get to the head's office, Jen was held up again. She saw the children out and caught Mrs Jones to let her know the outcome of her findings regarding the incident on the previous day between her son and Ian Williams. As was frequently the case, in her experience, Jen was not too surprised to find that Mrs Jones was not worried anymore. Johnny and Ian had become good friends again, and Mrs Jones was eager to get to the shops to get tea for her family organised. Jen then hurried along to the head's office.

"I believe I can do this role," Jen said as soon as she was settled in one of the chairs opposite Graham Lockwood. "The thing is, I haven't been here very long, and if you think I'm being presumptuous and there's no chance of me being ready for this promotion, I'd rather not go for it."

"Jen, you have made a very good start here. As you know, the observations of your classroom practice have been graded as very good, and with several elements of outstanding. Remind me how long you were in your last post."

"Three years," Jen responded.

"Well, it seems to me entirely appropriate that you put in an application, then. There may well be more than one person applying. Two others are interested and seeing me about it. Whether they'll both put in for it, of course, I have no idea yet. Time will tell."

Jen asked for some more information regarding the role, so that she could better judge what to include in her letter of application, but she was very encouraged by Graham's words.

"Some schools need a full-time post for this if they have mainly hard-to-reach parents, but here we have very few, as you know. However, we need someone to organise workshops, help remove barriers, encourage parents as co-educators and so forth."

Jen nodded, her mind already buzzing with ideas.

"I've prepared a paper, a sort of job description, but clearly the list could be endless. Give it some thought, and if you decide to apply I need the letter in by a week on Friday. There's no sense in hanging around."

"Thanks," said Jen, taking his paper. "That's put me in the picture well. I'm sure I'll be applying now."

Jen left the room, closing the door behind her. This sounded right up her street, and she was really excited by the thought of the endless possibilities. She knew she was personable and got on well with the parents, and she'd had some experience of working with outside agencies like social services and other provider groups in her previous placement. Now she was extremely keen to get home and share all the potential with

Mike. He would surely see the opportunities that this would provide for her.

When Jen got back to the classroom, Sally heard her arrive and popped her head round the door. She recognised the paper that Jen had in her hand.

"I've got one of those, but it seems like an awful lot of extra work to me."

"I don't know," said Jen. "It's exciting, and Graham said for the more major things like meetings with agencies there might be some classroom cover now and again. Otherwise it would be fitting it around everything else, certainly. You could do it though, I'm sure."

"I'm not certain I can do it just now, what with Mum and everything. She's on her own a lot as it is, and she's not getting any better. She's finding it increasingly difficult even to hold a cup."

On the way home, Jen had plenty to think about. She wanted to share her excitement with Mike. She was already planning things to include in her letter. It did seem as though Sally was going to pass up the opportunity, and she was genuinely sorry for her friend. She wondered who else might go for it.

On arriving home, Jen found the house in darkness. It felt decidedly chilly too, and somehow seemed unwelcoming. She switched on the wall lights and turned up the heating. As she drew the curtains and switched on the old-fashioned electric fire, the living room became a lot cosier. She wondered when Mike would be home, because she was hungry. He usually was back around this time, and so she started to prepare some pasta and a sauce. That would be quite quick, easy and tasty. By the time she had added the chorizo, mushrooms and onion, Jen's tummy was rumbling and she was beginning to wonder where Mike was.

Time dragged on. She decided to eat alone and then put the plates and pans in the dishwasher. Having been elated with the thought of the new role at work, Jen now felt deflated. She had so wanted to share the possibilities with Mike and get his opinion on the job prospects. Where was he? She decided to get the job description and make some notes.

A full hour later, Jen had more than three full pages of ideas that would help her to form a clear letter of application. Looking at the clock, she was surprised how late it had become. She was becoming seriously worried about Mike's absence and started to imagine all sorts of gory details, worrying herself even more. It was now eight o'clock, and still there was no sign and no word. He had his mobile phone. Why had he not used it? Had his car gone off the road and no-one had noticed? Maybe he was injured somewhere and the hospital or police hadn't had time to inform her. She spoke firmly to herself before her imagination got out of hand. *Maybe he's working and has forgotten the time. Or maybe he's gone for a drink with one of his work mates. But why has he not telephoned me?*

She started to consider who she might call to see if she could track him down, but then their friends would start to worry too. The police wouldn't be at all interested yet.

It was after nine o'clock when she finally heard the key in the lock.

"Hi!" called Mike, as if it was three hours ago.

"I imagined you lying in a ditch or on life support at the hospital," Jen exploded. "Where have you been?"

"What do you mean, where have I been?" Mike answered belligerently, all signs of jauntiness disappearing.

"Mike, I was really worried," Jen said more calmly. "I thought you must have had an accident."

"I only went to the gym. I met somebody I know and stayed for a swift half."

"But you always come home first and you almost never stay on in the bar." Jen took a deep breath and plastered on a smile. "Who did you meet?"

"Just a friend," Mike responded in a desultory fashion. "You needn't start checking up on me."

"I wasn't checking up," Jen said, feeling aggrieved. "I was worried! For goodness' sake, you are never this late without phoning me."

"Well, there's a first time for everything," Mike rasped back and stormed out of the room.

Jen sat down heavily. Tears came to her eyes. She didn't understand what was going on here at all.

# CHAPTER 10

When Jen went to bed, Mike seemed to be asleep. She wondered if he was pretending, but she wasn't prepared to continue the argument, so she quietly undressed and climbed in beside him. It was a long time before sleep came. She tossed about but couldn't relax enough to drop off as he seemed to have done. Silently, she got up again and went downstairs to make some warm milk. She sat in the living room, sipping it and thinking. Eventually she yawned and climbed the stairs to try sleeping again. It was some time later that she finally dropped into an exhausted slumber.

She awoke early and patiently waited for Mike to wake too. When he did open his eyes, she was tired again, but there was no time to go back to sleep. They looked at each other, and Jen broke the silence.

"Are we friends again?"

"I wasn't aware that we weren't friends," Mike answered.

This threw Jen, since they had gone to sleep on a blazing row. "Okay, let's just forget it, then," she said. There was a lot more to be said, but Mike was clearly not prepared to talk.

Jen got out of bed and headed for the shower. By the time she had finished, Mike had risen too. Downstairs, each of them got something to eat in a stilted manner. Jen made Mike a conciliatory cup of tea. He thanked her politely, took a couple of sips and said he had to go. He kissed her briefly on her cheek. She was at a loss to know what to do and started analysing her reactions from the previous evening. This continued as she collected her things, left the house and drove to work.

Once she arrived, however, she became immersed in the activities of the day and time flew by as normal. Thank goodness for a job she loved and that was so full-on she didn't have time to dwell on her uneasiness. By lunchtime, she was feeling much better. Before going to the staffroom, Jen called next door to see if Sally was ready to eat.

"I feel like congenial company today," said Jen. "I'm a bit fed up with the terrible twosome having a snipe at every opportunity."

Sally grinned in her usual upbeat way. "Let's go, then. I'm feeling good today and ready for anyone."

"What's the 'good', then?" Jen was curious.

"I've got a date this weekend," Sally divulged as she gave a beaming smile. "You'll never guess who."

"Don't keep me in suspense!"

"None other than Mr Christopher Mayhew," Sally said with delight.

Jen was a little surprised but nevertheless pleased for her friend. Thoughts of exchanged glances and brief conversations that she had witnessed flitted through Jen's mind. She was also pleased that Christopher was socialising again after all he had been through.

"Good for both of you," Jen said warmly. "So what are you doing, or where are you going?"

"Well, of course, there's Charlie to think of. On Saturday, I'm meeting them both at the café in the park to start with, and we'll take it from there."

"I really hope you have a good time and it works well." Jen meant it. "Changing the subject, have you decided whether to go for this internal promotion? If you'd rather not say, that's fine."

"I have decided," Sally answered. "I'm definitely not going for it. I feel I have so much on my plate at the moment with Mum and other personal stuff. I really don't think I could do it justice. You're the best candidate by a mile, so good luck to you if you're applying."

"Thanks," answered Jen.

After school, Jen was just packing up her bags, having prepared most of the classroom for the following day, when there was a knock on the door. She turned as it opened, and Christopher Mayhew walked in with Charlie in tow.

"I just popped in to say that we saw the doctor at the hospital again today. He's very pleased with Charlie's progress and is confident that he'll be fine for part-time school next week."

"That's excellent news," Jen said. She crouched down to Charlie's height to speak to him. "I'm really looking forward to having you back in our class, and so are the other children. They've missed you a lot."

He beamed at her, and when she rose and turned to Christopher, she saw the same large smile reflected on his face too. She could certainly see the father-son resemblance. Christopher had a kind, comfortable face with fine green eyes that twinkled when he smiled. The crinkles at the corners told Jen that for a long time during his life he must have smiled a lot. Of course, Charlie's rounded baby face had not yet acquired the chiselled features of his father's, and Charlie's curls were paler than his dad's attractive wavy brown hair. Christopher was clearly loyal and hardworking, and she could understand Sally being attracted to him.

When Jen arrived home, she was immediately transported back to the atmosphere of the previous night and even this morning, which had not been good. She followed her routine upon arrival, making the house warm and cosy now that it was dark so early and the wind was bitingly cold outside. Eventually, Mike came home too, but instead of rushing to meet him, she waited until he came into the living room.

"Hi," she said as normally as possible, feeling ridiculously nervous.

"Hi," he replied. "Have you started dinner, or shall I get on with it?"

"I haven't got that far yet. I've only just got in too."

"Okay, I'll crack on with it then," he said.

It was as if nothing had happened the previous night. They took it in turns to cook, so it was not particularly conciliatory for Mike to prepare dinner. Had Jen placed too much importance upon their words of the previous evening? Had she imagined the atmosphere this morning?

Following their meal, during which they chatted about their respective days, Mike turned on the television and Jen got out some school work — children's writing that she was going to mount for a wall display. She could have left it for Jodie, her teaching assistant, but she thought she might as well get it done so that Jodie could put it up the next day.

As she was sticking and trimming the work, the landline telephone rang. Since she was closer to it, she picked up the receiver to hear Diana at the other end.

"It's been such a long time since we saw each other," Diana said following the usual greetings. "I bumped into Mike the other day and we talked about dinner one evening. I've spoken to Pat, and she and Doug can come a week on Saturday. She says they can get a babysitter, one of the swimming teachers at Doug's work. Can you do then too?"

"A week on Saturday," Jen said out loud, turning to Mike and raising her eyebrows in a question. "It's Diana," she added, waggling the phone at him. "That sounds great, just hang on while I double-check Mike has nothing on then." Mike nodded agreement and turned back to the TV.

"I'm imagining Mike with 'nothing on' now." Diana laughed and before Jen could think of a response, she chattered on. "I wasn't sure if Pat and Doug would make it," she continued. "When I asked her, she seemed quite distracted."

"She's had some problems lately," Jen said obscurely.

"I know about all that," Diana said. "Why she doesn't just confront Doug if she's not happy, I don't know."

"She assured me she was going to, but I think she's frightened to do that," Jen said.

She had spoken to Pat just a couple of days ago, so she knew that her friend had not followed through. When she had arrived home that Saturday morning, Doug had been out, so her newfound resolve had faded away. When he returned with paint for the boys' bedroom and plans to build a toy chest, she began to wonder if it was over and the need for confrontation was past. He also wanted to discuss the possibilities of upgrading the windows.

"If he's planning long-term house improvements, then surely he's got over his distraction," she had said to Jen. Jen didn't understand how Doug could kid himself he was a happy family man and still mess around behind Pat's back.

"Anyway, it'll be lovely to see you all. We haven't done that for a while now," Jen said, to bring that part of the conversation to a close. "Do you want me to bring anything?"

"Oh, no. Our treat this time," said Diana generously. "Bring a bottle, if you want."

"Yes, of course, we'll do that." Jen laughed. "We'll probably walk round so we don't need to worry about drinking and driving."

Diana and Greg lived about twenty minutes' walk away from Mike and Jen. It was a large flat in an old, converted building which they'd rented together for about five years. They hadn't yet formalised their relationship, but as there were no children there seemed no pressing rush.

Jen liked Diana for her kindness and liveliness. You didn't have to work too hard when Diana was around, since she was spirited and sometimes seemed eccentric. Her long, auburn hair, her buxom figure, and her larger than life personality made her attractive and easy company. She was often outlandish in what she said and did, but she somehow seemed to get away with it.

Greg was slightly older than the others, but he was a gentle man with grey eyes and a quiet smile. He was the exact opposite of Diana in many ways, and he was often content to sit and let her take centre stage. Their relationship seemed to work. Jen liked Greg as well; he was dependable, kind and caring — and always trustworthy.

# CHAPTER 11

The day of the dinner party came around quickly. Jen was looking forward to going out that evening. It had been a while since the six of them had got together, and Diana and Greg were always good company.

Jen decided on something warm to wear. She felt she needed to be cosy, especially if they were walking to their friends' flat. The weather had a typical late autumn chill. She chose a chunky sweater with a large collar in a rich, deep rust colour that went well with her mid-length skirt and brown boots. She knew that the colour warmed her skin tone and the cut of the skirt was flattering. By the time she had done her hair and make-up and added a pair of long earrings, she felt good to go.

Both she and Mike wrapped up in their long coats. Ready to go, they stepped out into the cold. Their breath clouded as they walked. The sky was filled with stars, partially obscured by the streetlights.

Jen remembered their last holiday. They'd had a long weekend in the Dales at a small bed and breakfast that they had found as they drove. It had been a good choice with excellent, filling food, heavy old-fashioned furniture and a thick, cosy duvet on the big bed. The stars had been so bright and easy to see. They'd sat on a little terrace with a bottle between them. Jen had put her head back and sighed deeply with contentment. She remembered it clearly. Although it had only been earlier this year, it seemed like a long time ago.

Now, with heads down, they hurried along the road towards their target. They could have got a lift with Doug and Pat, but he was collecting their sitter, so they decided to work up an appetite with the brisk walk. They were pleased to arrive and greeted Greg with wide smiles when he opened the door. They handed over the clinking bag they had brought with them.

"One bottle of white and some beers." Mike smiled.

"Let the party begin, then," said Greg, taking their coats. They went through to greet Pat and Doug.

"Hiya, you two," Mike said. Doug stood and shook his hand and leant in to kiss Jen on her cold cheeks. Pat rose too and gave Jen a quick, firm hug and kissed Mike hello.

"It's really chilly out there," said Mike, rubbing his hands together.

"Did you walk?" Greg came back into the room.

"Yes, safer that way. Can't afford to lose my licence at the moment. Need the work, need the money. Mind you, with Jen's earnings I could become a 'kept' man."

Jen glanced across at him, but she could detect no malice in his comment this time.

Just then, Diana appeared from the kitchen. "Hello both of you." She embraced them both at the same time. "Well, you two haven't been to hell and back. You're freezing. Come and sit on the sofa by the fire, and Greg will sort out drinks. You look cosy, Jen, and lovely too."

Unlike Jen, Diana could have been dressed for summer. Her off-the-shoulder gathered blouse was bright red, a brave colour that enhanced the shades of her hair. She wore several heavy gold chains around her neck. Her skirt was a modest length, but when she sat down the high split revealed a good pair of legs.

"Just as well I don't have to go out tonight," she laughed, looking down at herself.

"We came in the car," said Doug. "One of us has to take the babysitter home later. I imagine it will be me. I doubt Pat will be able to drive later."

"Well, I do believe it's my turn, so I *shall* probably make the most of it," Pat said, not smiling. "I'm sure I can abstain if you insist, though."

"What can I get everyone to drink?" Greg busied himself with the task while everyone made casual conversation to cover the awkward pause that had followed the short exchange between Doug and Pat.

After a while, Diana announced that dinner must be ready and disappeared into the kitchen.

She called them to be served, and they all went across to the dining area where the table was lit up with candles. The light bouncing off the glassware, cutlery and warm colour of the mahogany table with the scarlet serviettes, gave the area a convivial glow as they all sat. It occurred to Jen that the colours mirrored Diana herself, making her seem radiant as well.

Jen considered herself an adequate cook, but the smell emanating from Diana's kitchen was wonderful and Jen had no doubt something special would arrive at any moment. The starter was not only delicious but looked amazing too. The warm goat's cheese on bruschetta was just the right depth of flavour, and the lightly baked figs and cool salad leaves with dressing looked and tasted perfect with it.

"Figs," Mike said. "Where on earth did you get those at this time of year? You're always so clever."

Everyone complimented Diana and conversation flowed with the wine. There was some slight awkwardness when Doug pointed out that the last starter that Pat had produced was not a patch on this one, but she laughed it off well.

"So Mike, have you been toning up your muscles much at the gym?" asked Diana. "I rather think you have." She laughed, pleased to see the look of awkwardness on his face.

He glanced at Jen and then carried on the banter with some restraint, Jen observed. Everyone else laughed indulgently. Diana liked nothing better than stirring up an atmosphere and seeing how people reacted. Mostly it was entertaining, but on this occasion Jen felt Mike's discomfort and was uneasy herself.

The evening progressed. Diana and Greg had really gone to town on both food and drink. Doug tried to impress everyone with his wine knowledge, but everyone took the mickey. This was so typical of Doug, and they were all used to it. He took it in good part generally.

Mike was unusually quiet, and Jen asked him if he was okay while there was a general milling around between the starter and main courses.

"I'm fine," he answered.

Following a hefty portion of delicious chicken cacciatore and vegetables that were served al dente, no one felt much like moving.

Diana was her normal dynamic self, and there was a lot of laughter between her and Doug and Greg. Normally Mike would have joined in while Pat and Jen were content to sit back and listen or laugh, knowing that they couldn't compete with this level of banter. This evening, he seemed reticent.

There was the odd snipe between Pat and Doug too, when the teasing seemed a bit near the knuckle.

During the chocolate crème brûlée dessert, Jen said, "This is truly delicious. I could get used to eating like this, but I'd be like a balloon in no time at all."

Doug responded with, "Pat keeps trying to lose weight, but it keeps finding her."

Diana took the sting out by applying the comment to herself.

Pat re-joined Doug's comment with, "To belittle is to be little."

Everyone laughed, but it seemed unaccustomed and false.

After dinner, with the coffee, they played cards for a while with tokens and matchsticks, but it was somewhat desultory. Eventually the evening broke up, with Pat announcing they had to get the babysitter home and Doug yawning and saying he had to be up early anyway.

Jen and Mike re-wrapped for their walk home but accepted the lift offered by Doug. They were all quiet in the car.

"Speak to you soon," said Jen as she and Mike got out.

"Cheers," said Mike. "Doug, I'll give you a call about that squash game, you know, the one we spoke about the other day."

"You didn't say you'd thought of playing squash," Jen said as they walked up the path. The way Mike had reminded Doug sounded a bit conspiratorial.

Once indoors, Jen and Mike took off their coats.

"I'm tired and ready for bed," said Mike.

"Me too," Jen replied. "That was a good meal, but there were too many undercurrents in the atmosphere, weren't there?"

Mike didn't reply.

"You were quiet tonight. Did you feel the atmosphere too?"

"It seemed fine to me. I told you earlier, I was fine."

"Well, Pat and Doug were on edge."

"I suppose so," Mike agreed in a half-hearted way.

He clearly knew exactly what was going on but wasn't prepared to share much, even with Jen. "Diana was on form, as usual," Jen continued. "Did she embarrass you when she commented about you working out and toning up at the gym? You were very non-committal about that one."

"I told you, I'm fine with it all. I wasn't quiet, I'm not ill, I'm quite alright," Mike snapped.

"Hey," Jen said. "I don't mean anything by it. I was only making conversation about the evening."

"I'm just a bit tired now, that's all," Mike said, heading up the stairs.

Thinking to change the subject, Jen asked Mike about the squash session as they climbed the stairs.

Mike sighed loudly. "It's not finalised yet, just an idea that Doug and I were talking about. As soon as it is, I'll check it out with you. Okay?"

Jen still tried hard to make conversation. Perhaps it was the wine talking and maybe she should have left it there, but she desperately wanted reassurance.

# CHAPTER 12

Jen was looking forward to Charlie's re-introduction to school. Having him back in her class would be lovely, but she was also a little apprehensive. She wasn't sure how the other children would react to the sight of his injury. She remembered her response and the expression on Sally's face when they'd seen his partially shaved head and livid scars. Children could be very, very kind and considerate to those in need, but they could also speak without thinking, and any comments could be hurtful and unhelpful to Charlie's self-esteem.

In addition, she was slightly unsure of his capabilities and how tired he might become. Still, all that would become clear. She would be in regular contact with Christopher and he would be on the end of the phone should there be any problems or questions. The meeting that she'd had with him and Graham Lockwood had been helpful and the paper from the hospital, via the nurse, had been informative.

For morning playtime, Jen walked towards the staffroom with Sally.

"I'm dying to know how you got on with your date on Saturday afternoon," she said at the first opportunity. "You met at the café in the park didn't you?"

Sally answered with animation, her eyes shining and her blonde ponytail bobbing as she walked. "We had a really great time. I was a bit nervous. It's a long time since I had a date, and with Charlie there too it had the potential to be tricky. I took along some bread for the ducks and geese, and we all fed those for a time. Charlie was quiet to start with, but after chucking bread he loosened up a bit. Mind you, those birds can be quite aggressive. He was understandably a bit nervous and was jumping about and running away. He's certainly lively enough again," she said. "We went inside for a coffee after that. They have a small display of flora and fauna and some push-button and feel-in-the-box activities for children, so we did those together. Charlie was chatty and fun by then. He seems quite well, now. It's amazing. So actually he helped break the ice. I really felt Christopher and I made a good connection. I talked for ages really easily."

"Did he tell you about his wife?" Jen asked. "I think it was breast cancer about three or four years ago."

"No, we didn't touch on much personal stuff. Just chatter really. I guess that'll come. It's quite hard for both of us, I think."

"Of course, you've got plenty of time. That all sounds great," Jen responded warmly. Perhaps her concerns for Sally were going to be unfounded, although she noted that Sally had said *she* chatted easily rather than 'we'. "Are you seeing him again?"

"Yes, he's asked me to go to the cinema with him next weekend. He told me he hasn't been for literally years, but his mum is going to come and take Charlie back to her house for the day and he's going to sleep there," Sally answered.

"Wow!" Jen exclaimed.

"It doesn't mean anything much," Sally said hastily. "I shan't be late out because I have to get Mum to bed."

"Of course," said Jen, "but you can still have a good evening without Christopher being too anxious about Charlie."

"Yes, I'm really looking forward to it. We seem to get on really well and have such a lot in common."

After playtime, a typically busy morning followed. Jen was hungry by the time she entered the staffroom again at lunchtime. She just had half an hour to eat her packed lunch, have a quick coffee and meet the children out on the playground for the afternoon session. Mary and Lesley were in their corner and several others were arriving at the same time as Jen. There was a general mêlée as people got themselves hot drinks. Jen joined Sally and shared some casual conversation about the morning while she ate.

The room was emptying again when the next conversation ensued. As it turned out, Jen was grateful for this. She had just finished her apple and rose to throw the core away.

"Right, time to get back, I guess." She was thinking about Charlie's return again and wondering how he would settle into the routines of the classroom after such a long and disruptive break, when a voice piped up from the corner.

"It's Mike, isn't it — your husband?" Mary enquired.

"Yes, that's right," Jen responded, wondering where this was leading.

"Tall, dark hair, red swimming shorts?"

"Yes," Jen confirmed.

"I thought it must be him," Mary added enigmatically. "I only met him that day he dropped you off for your interview, but I thought it was him — I saw him in the swimming pool at the leisure centre on Saturday morning."

"He quite often goes to the gym there," said Jen as pleasantly as possible. "He's turning into a real fitness enthusiast."

"Well, he certainly looked enthusiastic," Mary said. "It wasn't keeping fit he was particularly interested in, I wouldn't have said."

"What do you mean?" Jen could no longer resist asking.

"The curvaceous redhead seemed to be taking his enthusiasm readily enough," Mary couldn't help smiling.

Jen felt her breath leave her body in a rush and her heart pounded erratically. Then she managed to restrain herself and respond calmly. "He told me he'd met Diana. She's a good friend to both of us. We had dinner with her and her partner just this weekend."

All this time, Lesley, Mary's only real supporter, looked down at her hands in her lap and refused to be drawn into the conversation. It seemed that she drew the line at some things.

As she headed back up the corridor to her classroom, Jen felt quite shaken. She didn't believe Mike would have overstepped any lines, but she was really angry that Mary had seen fit to be so spiteful. Perhaps she had guessed she would be applying for the internal promotion and felt it might be a way to put Jen down and make her feel less confident. If Jen wasn't careful, she could let this nasty intimation affect her, just as Mary was hoping. She wasn't going to let herself fall for it, she thought with determination.

As Jen arrived in her classroom, she headed for the outside door onto the playground. It was nearly time for the whistle, and children were tidying away the play equipment. She could see her teaching assistant, Jodie, shepherding children in various directions, because Jodie was also the senior midday supervisor. Jen went outside to meet the children and take them into the classroom from the playground.

Most children stayed at school for lunch, but one or two went home and Jen greeted their parents with a sunny smile as she welcomed all the children in. Christopher Mayhew was there too, with Charlie. The little boy was wearing a baseball cap so the full extent of his recovering injury was masked. All thoughts of the horrid lunchtime conversation evaporated instantly. Her mind turned to that morning when she had spoken to her class about his imminent return and described how he might look. She didn't want the shock of that to provoke unwanted comments from the children.

Several of her class and one or two from Sally's parallel class were clustered around Charlie and his dad on the playground. As the whistle went for the children to line up, several tried to take his hand. Jen was well aware that some of the children, both older and younger ones, would try to 'mother' him. There were several issues for which she might need to be ready.

Charlie's scars looked less raw now, and his dad must have taken him to the barber because he sported a very short but much more even haircut. His adorable curls had all gone now, so the shaved part was significantly less noticeable than when Jen had visited his home with Sally. He had suddenly lost his baby look and seemed older. However, he leaned against Jen as his dad spoke.

"He's been really looking forward to this afternoon," Christopher said as Jen greeted him.

He bent to kiss his son goodbye and indicated he should join the line. After the lad had moved away, Christopher added, "I'll be on the end of the phone if you need me at all."

Jen quite understood his anxiety and made to reassure him. "I know you'll be there, but I'm sure he'll be fine. Try not to worry, although I'm sure you will anyway."

They laughed together for a moment, each understanding the other. With that, the whistle went and it was time for the afternoon session to begin. Christopher spotted Sally in the distance and raised his hand, just a little, before he turned and headed for the side of the school and the gate.

Jen took her class indoors and as they hung up their jackets and hats, she hovered in the doorway to ensure good order. The children knew her expectations now and responded positively to her calming comments. As they came to sit on the carpet ready for registration, she caught several children staring at Charlie's head, but no-one said anything.

Jen had decided to bite the bullet and have it out in the open, so after saying good afternoon to each child as she called their names, she welcomed Charlie back to the classroom. As the hospital leaflet suggested, she had decided to let Charlie talk about his time in hospital and allow the others to ask some questions if they wanted. This should demystify the experience for all of them and help Charlie to feel accepted.

Some questions were very perceptive. Charlie spoke openly and with confidence. Jen didn't allow them to dwell too long, though, before she moved the session on.

They all had a good afternoon. Charlie didn't need anything in particular. The other children, having had the opportunity to talk, carried on and ignored his looks. They had no PE, and at playtime he stayed indoors with Jen. They read a book together and then he wanted to play with some of the classroom toys. Since playtimes were unwinding times for children, she was content to leave him to his own devices for a while. She got on with her own work, companionably silent.

By the time the afternoon was over, Jen was confident that Charlie was going to continue to flourish at school. She took her class to the door after she had waited for each child to do their own coat up and collect their things, and then let them out to meet their parents and carers. Christopher was there to greet Charlie, and having given him a hug he came towards Jen.

"Come in," she said, holding the door wider. "I shan't be a minute. I just need to make sure they're all collected." She indicated the remaining children.

Two minutes later, she joined him in the warmth of the classroom.

"The smell of these places always transports me back to my own schooldays," he said.

"Good days?"

"Hmm, not ever so," he replied. "I remember being scared of several teachers and hating the school toilets." He laughed. "So different here, for Charlie. He loves it, and you. How has he been today?"

Jen smiled at the compliment. "Charlie, would you go and put this away for me in the three bears home corner, please?" Jen asked the little boy so that he was out of earshot. She went on to explain that they had all shared a discussion about Charlie's accident and his stay in hospital. "I'm afraid I also took the opportunity for a bit of propaganda for promoting safety too. We talked about wearing bike helmets and road awareness. The Year 6 children do a bike course here at school, but accidents make me wonder if that's too late. He stayed indoors with me at playtime."

"I really don't want to put you to extra work," Christopher said, looking worried.

"I don't usually leave the classroom in the afternoon break," Jen explained. "When it's my turn for duty, one of the other teachers or our teaching assistant will look after him. He'll have to go onto the playground before too long, but this week it's probably better that he stays in. We'll stick to what we agreed about PE, and at the end of the week we'll decide how he's been and whether he's ready for all day."

"If we can take it as it comes, like we said, that would be great," Christopher responded. "I really can't thank you enough for your kindness."

"Really," Jen assured him, "it's a pleasure to help in any way. Are you ready to go home with your dad, Charlie? I was just telling him what we chatted about when you came into school after lunch. Have you had a good afternoon, do you think?"

Jen didn't want Charlie to think he was totally excluded from their discussion when it was about him.

Charlie carried on chattering away to his dad as they moved towards the internal door and up the corridor to the front entrance. Jen followed them through the door and stood talking to them both on the step for several minutes. Conversation flowed between the three of them very easily, and there was quite a bit of laughter too.

"Oh, I almost forgot, I've nearly finished the book you leant me," Jen said.

Charlie had drifted away to the footpath and was kneeling down, peering into the flowerbed. A further conversation ensued between Jen and Christopher about the book, and then they joined Charlie to discover what he was looking at, sharing his interest in an exceedingly long worm.

Eventually, they all stood and said their goodbyes. Jen reassured Christopher that she would keep in touch and he thanked her again.

She shivered as she turned to the front door. It was very wintery, and she had stood chatting without her coat on, not realising how cold it was. She thought she would collect a warming cup of tea to take back to the classroom, so she headed for the staffroom. When she arrived, Sally was there before her.

"Hello," Jen said to her friend. "I've just been chatting to Christopher about Charlie, but it's really cold out there."

"I saw you," Sally stated. "I thought he might have popped in to say hello to me too."

"I guess his mind was on Charlie. I think that's understandable, though," Jen said equably.

"Well, of course, but he could have just said hello, all the same," Sally persisted.

Jen tried hard to think of a way to phrase what she was thinking. "Sometimes it's hard to separate work from personal stuff. I'm sure he was seeing this visit as work." She tried to be diplomatic, referring to Christopher rather than Sally herself.

"You and he looked like you were getting along well, though," Sally observed, sounding worried.

"He's just a worried parent of a poorly little boy in my class," Jen reassured her friend. Changing the subject and trying to sound positive, she asked, "What are you going to see at the weekend when you go to the pictures?"

"I don't know yet, we still need to decide. I looked up the cinema on the internet last night to see the synopses and times. Perhaps I'll catch him tomorrow and ask what he fancies seeing," Sally answered, brightening.

That evening, Jen still had to finalise her letter of application for the internal promotion. The pages of notes she had made previously were a help, but she needed to be concise.

Rumour had it there would be one other candidate. Sheila had dropped that much information to her, although she hadn't said who. All would become clear after the closing date, but Jen thought the only other likely candidate could be Mary. With the end of her pen tapping her cheek, Jen contemplated the prospect. Mary had been at the school for quite a while and as one of the older, established members of staff, it was a little surprising that she had not thought of promotion before, despite the fact that she had the knowledge. Maybe her people skills left something to be desired, and that was the crux of this job.

As Jen finished her application letter, she asked Mike to read it and check it over for her. There would be nothing worse than making a foolish spelling error.

"I think the job is yours. Having read this, how could they even think of giving it to one of the gruesome twosome, even if she applies?"

"It all needs to be accurate. I can't blag any evidence like I could if I was applying from another school. They know me and exactly what I can and have done. Do you think it's concise enough?"

"Yes," he answered. "It's a good letter, like I say. I think it's yours."

Jen smiled at Mike's praise. She had sometimes shared Mary's gems with him. "You'll never guess her latest pearl of wisdom." Jen launched into the story of the staffroom discussion from earlier, making it clear to Mike that she knew he wouldn't do anything wrong with their mutual friend.

"Ridiculous," he barked. Reaching down to the side of the sofa, he retrieved his newspaper and dived behind it, from where he said, "The woman should be locked up."

Jen almost jumped at his response, but she guessed he must be quite angry, as she had been.

# CHAPTER 13

The day of the interview dawned and had the promise of being bright and clear. The wind seemed to have died at last and the day before had been beautiful, if cold. *This must be a good omen*, thought Jen.

She knew now that she and Mary were the only candidates for the internal promotion. She felt confident, but nothing was guaranteed and so she would still need to do the best interview she could. This was also necessary for her pride. She wanted to know she had been given the job on proper merit and not by default. Also, as an internal candidate, pressure seemed greater because she couldn't just walk away if she wasn't given the job.

She was awake early and tried to clear her mind of the imaginary conversations that were whizzing around in her brain. No matter how many of these she had, rationally, she knew that no part of the interview would follow her prepared fictional route. Jen didn't want to wake Mike up early, so she crept out of bed. Downstairs, she pushed the kitchen door closed and filled the kettle. As she waited for it to boil, she re-read her letter of application. She didn't need to go into school as normal, so she had plenty of time to prepare. She had left everything ready for the supply teacher and as her surname, Lucas, came after Mary's alphabetically, she knew her interview was second. By lunchtime, it would all be over. Whichever way it went, an afternoon of normal teaching would take her mind off it, and she could be at home with Mike to await the result. Graham had said he would telephone by early evening so that the two candidates had time to adjust before seeing everyone at school again.

Mike staggered downstairs three quarters of an hour later. "You were up early," he noted. "Why was that?"

"Couldn't get interview questions out of my head," Jen responded.

"Oh, yes. I forgot. What time have you got to be there?"

"My interview isn't until ten-thirty, so I've got ages yet," Jen replied.

How could Mike have forgotten this important day? *Oh well,* she thought, *he seems to have a lot on his mind.* He remembered to wish her well as he left for work.

When she arrived at school, Jen began to feel really nervous. She knew this was irrational because she already had a job here, one she enjoyed. It was no desperate thing for her to be doing, but she liked the idea of this role and it was one she knew she could do well. If Mary, of all people, got the position over her, she knew she would be devastated.

She let the secretary know she had arrived, and then she entered the staffroom which, thankfully, was empty. Some kind person, Sheila, she imagined, had left a coffee pot with milk, a plate of biscuits and pretty paper serviettes on a tray as a welcome. This was not normal fare for the staffroom and Jen appreciated the touch, making a mental note to thank the deputy head. She hadn't been sitting for more than about ten minutes when she heard movement in the corridor. This was sooner than she had expected. Thank goodness she had come early.

As the door opened, Jen's heart skipped a nervous beat. She hadn't touched the coffee, but knew she would be ready for it when she came out of the interview. She didn't want to risk needing the loo during the questioning.

A head popped around the door and the chair of governors, Mr Davies, said, "Hello, Jen. I know we're early and if you want another few minutes, that would be fine. Equally, we can get straight on with it if you like."

Jen had met David Davies at her last interview, and he had been at the school, wandering round, on the evening of the parent-teacher consultations. He had some fairly senior position at the post office, and he also had a child in year four. She liked him. He was friendly and certainly seemed to know his stuff.

"I'd really like to get on with it," Jen replied.

"Are you feeling nervous?"

"I am a bit, this time," Jen said.

"Well, there are no trick questions," he said easily, as he led the way to the head's office. "We just want to find out how you see this role progressing and what you can bring to it."

He held the door to Graham Lockwood's office open for her. As she entered, Graham stood and welcomed her, indicating where she should sit. She put down her bag and made sure she placed her bottom right back on the seat, trying to look relaxed.

"Thanks for coming, Jen," he said.

Once everyone was seated and opening welcomes had been voiced, the substance of the interview began. They wanted to know, of course, what Jen thought the role involved, and then they moved on to how she would implement some of her ideas. She managed to get the title of the recent Government document, 'Every Child Matters', into the conversation and was confident that her ideas would reflect the Ofsted inspectorate's framework. She was convinced that the work would need to be child-centred and that positive partnerships between home and school should support children's development and learning.

She knew that a parent needing support should be identified at the earliest stage of a child's schooling and that the family should be linked to specialised support if it was required. While all this was true, Jen was aware that it all sounded a bit bookish so, having pondered the thing at home for some time, she decided to add an anecdote to bring the theory into everyday reality.

She spoke of a family she had known at her previous school, where there had been twin girls. They had been vulnerable, having been fathered by their grandfather. Jen detailed the influence she'd had in obtaining external support for the mother and her twins, both of whom were underachieving in school and who appeared frail and uncared for. She was able to talk about her professional relationship with the family and the care she took to deal with the various elements of the case with sensitive efficiency. Although their mother clearly loved them both, she found it difficult to know how best to cater for their needs. It was a powerful story that illustrated Jen's ability to handle such delicate matters.

She was also able to speak at length about the children who attended her current school. She thought of those who had mild learning difficulties, and those whose parents wanted to support them but were unsure how. She had ideas for workshops and visits.

Finally the interviewers asked her if she had any questions for them, and Jen took the opportunity to gain further information about resources that might be available to her. She knew she would need a small amount of money and a little non-contact time to achieve all that she would like to do.

As the interview drew to a close, Jen hoped that she had done enough to get the job. She wanted to continue to support vulnerable families and to develop children in need, and with extra resources the possibilities would be far greater. She thanked the interviewers for the opportunity and left the room.

When she entered the staffroom to make a cup of tea, Jen found she was shaking. It must have been a reaction to the tension she'd been experiencing. She wanted, so much, to be able to do this. She had a little time before lunch, when the midday supervisors would arrive and others would enter the room, so she sat and went over the questions and her responses. She hoped she had done enough.

That evening, Jen left school in good time and decided to see Pat on her way home. She was ready to share a good chat and felt she would get more joy there than with Mike. She wanted to see how Pat was coping too. As she knocked on the door, she could hear the boys playing some wild game. It was more difficult for them to let off steam in a small house when the weather was poor.

Pat answered her knock just as a toy car came hurtling up the wooden floor of the hallway. Ben and Joe had their Hot Wheels track set up at the far end, and they were shrieking with excitement as the cars sped from the stunt ramp along the floor.

"Welcome to bedlam," Pat smiled and raised her voice above the noise.

"I just thought I'd come and see how things are and tell you about my day," replied Jen as she stepped around the game.

"You've had your interview, haven't you? I was going to ring you later, but it's better to chat face to face. I told you to let me know."

They went into Pat's kitchen and she put the kettle on.

"I think it's safest in here," Pat said. "We can chat because the boys are completely engrossed. They've had a snack, so they should be quite happy for a while and leave us to it. I wanted to tell you the latest as well." She looked away.

Jen immediately wondered if there had been further developments in Pat's situation and put her own news on hold, determined to give her good friend whatever support was necessary. As they settled at the kitchen table, Jen asked, "What's happened?"

"Doug's gone," Pat said bluntly.

Jen felt a mixture of shock and relief for her friend.

"Well, he's gone to stay with a guy who works at the leisure centre with him, just for a time, anyway. I suppose it's what people call a trial separation. I told him to go," Pat added, almost as if she was surprised by her own decision.

"I can't help feeling it's a good thing, for now, anyway," Jen replied. "It should give you both some time to consider things. How are you coping?" Jen privately thought Pat looked better for it already.

"Oh, alright, I suppose."

"What have you told the boys?"

"I'm afraid I've just said that their dad is on a course and can only visit at the weekend. I told them it will be for a short while."

"So what prompted you? I know it can't have been easy," Jen said.

"To be honest, it's a bit of a relief. You were right, Jen. It was all making me ill, and that wasn't good for the boys, was it? There's no doubt that he was shocked. I'm not sure whether that was because I had found out or because I actually told him to go. He kept saying how sorry he was and that he loved us. Right at this moment, though, I'm not sure I know what love is."

"Pat, I'm so sorry. If there's anything that I can do, you must just ask. Whether it's babysitting or listening, or anything else."

"I know, Jen, and just knowing that helps a lot."

"What do you think will happen?" Jen wanted to know. She knew it was slightly more complicated when children were involved, but she also thought Pat was better off without Doug. To her, it seemed a simple decision.

"I'm hoping the shock will be enough for him to really consider whether he will be better off on his own — or with her, I should say, and whether the grass really is greener. It still needs cutting and tending, even on the other side of the fence." Pat managed a half-smile.

Jen could see that it was a struggle. She couldn't understand how Pat could really consider having Doug back after the way he had treated her, although it seemed such a sad thing for a marriage to falter like this. Perhaps it hadn't been such a good relationship in the first place. Thank goodness she could rely on Mike, even if they did have the odd spat.

Pat asked how the interview had gone.

"Well," said Jen, "I really do want this job now I've put in this much effort, and the thought of Mary getting it has also spurred me on. I just hope I've done enough."

"I should be very surprised if you don't get it, if that's the only opposition," said Pat.

Ben had been in Mary's class the previous year, and while he liked her well enough and had progressed satisfactorily, Jen knew that Pat had not particularly liked parents' evenings that year.

"I don't just want to get it because the opposition is duff, though," said Jen. "I'd like to think I got it because I'd earned it."

"Of course," said Pat. "But I don't think they would give it to anyone who didn't deserve it just because you work there. When do you expect to hear?"

"Someone is going to telephone this evening at around seven o'clock. That's a lot longer than it normally takes, but they thought that as we're both internal candidates it would be better to be told at home. We'll have time whichever way it goes to get over it before facing everyone. That'll be horrid for both of us, whoever gets it," answered Jen.

The boys appeared, having exhausted both the game they were playing and themselves.

"Can we put the television on now?" Joe, the younger but bolder one asked the question. No doubt he was put up to it by his older brother.

"Yes, you can," responded their mum, but having glanced up at the clock she added, "But only for half an hour and then it's tea, bath and bed. You need to sleep a bit earlier tonight." Turning to Jen, she explained that they had been out with Doug quite late the previous evening.

"It's typical in our situation, isn't it? He gets to do all the fun stuff and I get to be the ogre who says 'early to bed'. Still, I took them out for burger and chips the other night, just so they could see me giving a treat too. It's all so unnatural, though, and it can't be good for them." Pat looked worried.

"You're right, but it's early days, and you'll both find an equilibrium. So long as you both keep talking about that sort of thing and don't try to out-do each other," said Jen.

"You are wise," said Pat. "It's good to have a sounding board in you."

"Thank you," Jen replied warmly. "I guess I better make tracks and let you get on. Mike will be in before long."

"How are things there?"

"Alright, I suppose. He's a bit reticent at the moment and not keen to talk much. He really isn't enjoying his work, so I'm trying not to gloat too much about mine, like you suggested."

"Be careful about my advice." Pat smiled. "I'm not the world's best authority on married life, am I?"

When she got home, Jen realised it was going to be a long evening of waiting for the results of her interview. She tried to imagine how she would behave as she entered the staffroom the next day, whether she got the job or she didn't. What would she say to Mary? What would Graham Lockwood have to say to her? She supposed that the whole result thing would be a five-minute conversation piece at school, however it turned out — she hoped.

Then her mind turned to Mike. How would he react if she got the job? Would the extra money come between them, or would he be pleased to be able to redecorate the living room as she had suggested? Life seemed so complicated sometimes.

Jen glanced at her watch: five to six. She felt a moment of breathless panic as she thought about the phone call.

She was wondering what to do next to make the time pass when the sound of the telephone ringing broke into her thoughts. Oh my, was this it? It was a little early still.

She picked it up but was surprised to hear Greg's deep voice at the other end.

"Hi, honey," he said cheerfully.

"Hello," said Jen, wondering why Greg would be phoning her now and hoping she could get him off the line quickly. Graham might phone and find it engaged.

"I gather you had your interview today. How did it go?"

"Greg, how kind of you to ask. I think it was alright, but it's always difficult to know, isn't it? As I came out, I was thinking of other things I should have said."

"I think that's always the case, but it doesn't really mean anything. So when do you expect to hear? I thought you might already know."

"Normally they tell you pretty much straight away, but because it's an internal thing I'm expecting a phone call this evening at about seven," answered Jen.

"I'll get off the line in case they phone early. Good luck. I think you would do the new job really well. You've got such good people skills and you work hard, lovely girl. Let us know how you do, when you're ready, of course."

"Thank you, Greg, and thanks again for asking," Jen said, looking at her watch yet again.

She wandered into the kitchen, vaguely thinking about food. She reflected on the call and considered again what a gentle, considerate man Greg was.

It wasn't long before Mike arrived home. "So, how did it go?" he asked.

Jen remembered some of the questions she had been asked and tried to describe the answers she had given. "I really don't know if it's enough, though."

"Well, the opposition isn't up too much, is it?"

"I know, but they may give it to neither of us if they feel I wouldn't do it justice either," said Jen gloomily.

"Let's have dinner," said Mike. "You'll know soon enough, and then we can decide how to spend your millions." He smiled.

Jen was glad for his level-headed mood. She felt she couldn't have handled snide comments about earnings at this moment.

Shortly after finishing dinner and washing up, they settled in the living room in front of the television. Suddenly, Jen's mobile trilled and made her jump. She glanced at Mike and leapt to her feet, moving to the hallway.

"Hello, Jen," said a voice at the other end. It was her mum.

"Mum, I'll have to call you back. I'm really sorry, but I'm waiting for school to call with the results of my interview."

"Sorry, love. Let us know, darling, and good luck." The phone went dead and the call was ended.

Jen returned to the living room as Mike turned to her with raised eyebrows.

"It was Mum. Can you believe it? She was only calling to see what the result was," Jen responded, smiling again now. "What timing!"

Just then, her mobile rang again and Jen's heart thumped as she returned to the hallway.

"Hello, is that Jen Lucas?"

"Yes, hello," responded Jen.

"It's David Davies here," came a lilting voice at the other end. "Sorry to keep you waiting, Jen, but we have made a decision and the personnel committee of the Governors agree. We were very impressed with your answers and would like to offer you the job, Jen."

"Thank you so much," said Jen, breathing a huge sigh of relief. Suddenly, her legs felt wobbly.

"Yes, your answers were exceptionally mature and sensibly realistic, and so we have every faith in your abilities to take on this extra responsibility."

"Thank you," said Jen again, feeling tongue-tied.

"Graham will speak to you more in the next day or two, but in the meantime congratulations from us all on the Governing Body."

"I won't let you down," said Jen, feeling more and more ecstatic.

"Well, have a good evening, Jen. Speak soon. Bye."

"Goodbye."

She disconnected the call and bounced into the living room with a broad smile of relief and pleasure on her face. Mike turned as the door re-opened.

"I got it." Jen's eyes sparkled as she announced her good news. "I'm so relieved. I was beginning to talk myself into not being too disappointed if I was unsuccessful."

"Well done," said Mike. "So when does all the extra work start?"

"After Christmas, officially, but as soon as I like, I suppose. We'll be able to get that flatscreen television for over Christmas, though, won't we? I won't get the first increased paycheque until the end of January, but we'll know it's coming. I better phone Mum back. Shall we open that bottle of bubbly we've had for ages when I've done that? I shan't be long."

Jen went up to the bedroom to start telephoning several people, including Pat and Greg, whom she knew were also waiting to share her good news.

# CHAPTER 14

Once December arrived, everything at school seemed to be geared towards Christmas. Children's plays and concerts were a low-key affair these days, but songs still needed to be learned and while costumes and practices were restricted to the week before the event, the children's educational activities took on a festive nature.

Jen felt festive too, and one evening she decided to telephone Pat and Diana with the suggestion of a girl's day out at the health and beauty centre in a nearby town. She didn't want to go to the local leisure centre because that's where Doug worked. Jen had no desire to see Doug at the moment, and she knew that Pat would want to avoid him. She hoped the day out could be arranged for a Saturday when Pat's mum, or Doug, might take care of the boys. Maybe they could even have dinner out.

Looking online, Jen found a day's spa deal that included a glass of bubbly on arrival, a massage, a facial, and lunch. It sounded perfect.

Jen phoned Pat and discussed the idea. Pat sounded really excited about it and was sure her mum would have the boys if Doug couldn't or wouldn't.

"I'll call Diana then and book it, shall I?" asked Jen.

"It sounds really great. I'm looking forward to it already," Pat sighed.

Jen got straight on the phone to Diana. "Hi, Diana, it's Jen." She explained the planned outing.

"Well…" Diana hesitated. "I'm not sure. I've had a stonking cold and I still feel ropey."

"It's another week yet, and it sounds like just the sort of thing to pick you up again," said Jen cheerfully.

"You may be right, but I've got loads to catch up on, so I think I'll skip this time. Sorry."

"Oh!" said Jen, somewhat surprised. It was unlike Diana to miss something like this. She was usually the first to jump at such an opportunity. "Okay, then. Maybe next time."

After a few pleasantries, Jen said that she hoped she felt better soon and hung up. She rang Pat back to say that it would be just the two of them.

"That's fine," said Pat. "We can still talk the hind leg off a donkey, just you and me." She laughed.

That Saturday dawned dull, cold and grey, so Jen was pleased that she had booked their day out.

"What will you do today?" she asked Mike as she prepared to get out of bed.

"No plans," he answered vaguely, turning away as she got up.

There had been no more arguments, but Mike had seemed oddly distant. There were no reasons for this that Jen could put her finger on. They both were busy, and she knew Mike didn't enjoy his work. She supposed he was just tired, and the weather didn't encourage anyone to be lively. She had made an effort to be more understanding and had not talked about her success or satisfaction at work. Oh well. She was looking forward to this day.

She dressed quickly, and as she left the bedroom she said, "I'll see you at about six this evening. Are you going to the gym as usual? Have a good day yourself. Don't do too much."

"Mmm, okay," was all the response she got from his half-buried face.

Jen picked Pat up, and they made their way to the spa.

Their day lived up to all expectations. On arrival, having booked in, they were given fluffy towels and a tour of the facilities. After changing and snuggling into their thick robes, they were shown to a cosy area where they were offered glasses of fizz.

"This is decadent," Jen observed.

When they were ready, a lively young woman came to fetch them and took them to the sauna. She showed them how to operate the steam, suggested how long they should stay and left them to it. As they sat and soaked up the heat, Jen debated whether to ask Pat how she was doing. She didn't want to bring up the subject, since this was their escape day. After a few minutes, however, Pat started to speak.

"I'm hoping this separation will help Doug to see where his future lies." Pat shrugged.

"If he decides he wants to come back, what will you do?" asked Jen tentatively.

"I have to think of the boys."

"You have to think about you as well. If this were to happen yet again, you would be no good for the boys if you get ill," Jen offered.

"I know, but I'm under no illusions about marriage now, and under no delusions about my importance to Doug. If he comes back, at least I shall be less reliant upon him, emotionally. I can manage without him now, I think."

Jen was quiet for a moment while she contemplated whether to speak her mind or not.

Just then, the young woman returned and suggested they might like to have a swim and then shower. "Come through to the treatment rooms when you are ready," she added.

"This is just what the doctor ordered," said Pat as they stood under the steaming hot shower a little later.

After drying off, they donned their robes again and went through to a calm room with soft music playing in the background. It smelled clean and delicately perfumed. Jen had never had a scalp massage before, but she really enjoyed it. She felt herself sinking further into the inclined chair as she turned her face to the ceiling, closed her eyes and completely relaxed. Pat was next to her, and Jen wondered if she had dozed off.

As the day progressed, the two friends enjoyed a light lunch with a refreshing glass of Sauvignon Blanc, followed by a facial and haircare session.

When it was time to go home, Jen said, "That went so quickly, but I feel much better for it."

"Oh, so do I. What a fantastic idea it was, Jen. You're so clever," Pat said. "I feel all warm and relaxed. Ready to face whatever comes next."

When Jen dropped Pat off outside her gate, she was feeling more positive about things too. "I'm sure you'll cope with whatever happens, Pat."

"What about you?" asked Pat.

"I think Mike and I will be okay too. I'm more circumspect about work, and I give him my time as much as possible. His job will sort itself out, or he'll change, I suppose. Anyway, thanks for today too. I really enjoyed it."

Mike's car wasn't there when Jen pulled up, and she hoped he had found something good to do with his day too. She entered the house, went into the kitchen and having flung her swimming stuff in the washing machine, she put the kettle on.

Time passed, and still Mike wasn't home. Jen remembered the argument they'd had the last time he'd been late, and although she was uneasy she banished negative thoughts and busied herself with going to the bedroom and tidying up. She straightened the bed, smiling to herself at Mike's scruffiness. He had probably slept in, she thought indulgently, as she picked his dirty clothes off the floor and carried more washing downstairs to the kitchen. Stuffing it all into the machine, she switched it on and went to turn on some music.

She pushed her phone into the speaker to charge it and searched for something to listen to. Then she curled up in the corner of the sofa with her book. She was blowed if she was going to do work now. This was the book that Christopher had lent her and she was really enjoying it.

Reaching over to switch on the table lamp, her mind wandered to Christopher and his attractive green eyes with the crinkles at the corners. He was so like an older version of his adorable son. Charlie had made excellent progress and had started to come in on a full-time basis again. He was a real sweetie with his beaming smile and ready laugh; such a sunny personality. She smiled involuntarily to herself.

Just then, her mobile rang. Sighing, she stood to retrieve it from the docking station. "Hello," she answered.

"Oh, Jen, it's Greg," came a slightly surprised voice.

"Hello, Greg," Jen replied. "What can I do for you?"

"I wondered whether you'd finished your pamper day. It's getting on a bit, and I wondered where Diana was. I'm not exactly checking up, of course, but I was starting to get a bit worried as she said she'd definitely be back by four."

"Sorry, Greg, I haven't seen her."

"But I thought she was going with you today. I'm sure she said that."

"No, Greg, she cried off — she said she hadn't been well and had loads to do."

"I've obviously got my wires crossed," Greg replied. "Sorry to bother you."

"No problem, of course," Jen said. "Let me know if she doesn't reappear, won't you? I'm sure she's just forgotten the time at the shops or something." Jen automatically looked at her watch. It was well after six. "Perhaps she called in at the supermarket on her way home," she added.

"It'll be something like that," Greg said.

"Mike was really late home a little while ago," said Jen. "I gave him hell when he got back. We had a right old ding-dong about it, but it was only because I'd been worried. He'd only been at the gym, but I had him in a ditch or bleeding to death at A&E. I'm sure Diana will be back soon."

"I'm sure you're right. Sorry to bother you, darling," Greg responded.

"No bother, at all. Speak soon, Greg." Jen rang off.

Checking her watch again, Jen was just feeling uneasy herself when she heard Mike's key in the door. Being reminded of her reaction the last time, having just spoken to Greg about it, she was careful to smile. "Hello, have you had a good day?"

"Yes, I've had a really good day," said Mike, seeming very upbeat. "How about you?"

Jen did a twirl and touched her hair. Then she went on to give Mike the salient details of her session at the spa with Pat. "So what did you do?" she asked.

"Oh, just this and that," Mike answered. "I pottered around here and then went to the gym." He turned to leave the room. "I'm just going for a shower."

*He normally showers at the gym*, thought Jen uneasily, as she started to prepare dinner.

As they were eating, Jen told him about Greg's call. "He hasn't called back, so I suppose Diana must have turned up. Perhaps I'll ring him after dinner and see."

"What's he checking up on her for?" was Mike's response.

Aware of their argument, Jen tentatively suggested that perhaps he was just worried about her.

A noisy sigh escaped from Mike. "Maybe. Well, I bumped into her at the gym and she was fine, so he's just fussing."

"What? You saw her at the gym?" Jen creased her forehead. "That's odd, she said she couldn't join us today because she had been feeling poorly and had lots to do."

"Well, she wasn't using the gym, she was just there," he said vaguely. "Don't you start fussing, too."

"But..." She refrained from saying anything else, aware that she would be heading into fraught territory. She turned away before she could make matters worse and made an excuse to go to the lavatory.

She put the lid down and sat with her head in her hands. What was happening here? This wasn't right. She shouldn't be pussyfooting around Mike like this. It never used to be like it seemed to be now. Was she making matters worse by avoiding conflict, or should she come right out and have a blazing row? She sighed. It all seemed so complicated when it should be easy and safe and comfortable.

# CHAPTER 15

After an unremarkable week, with Jen and Mike edging carefully around each other at home, the following weekend dawned bright and clear, but very cold. Jen got up early on Saturday morning and decided she would have a thorough clear-out of the wardrobes. They both had old clothes and shoes cluttering the place, and with Christmas fast approaching she should make space. She knew Mike would be going to the gym as he usually did on a Saturday morning, so as soon as he had left she collected binbags and dusters and set to work.

She started on her wardrobe. It was a satisfying task, and by the time her half was completed she was pleased with the results. After a much-needed cup of tea, she decided she would make a start on Mike's half, putting the stuff she wasn't sure about to one side.

She found several old T-shirts and shirts and was just deciding what to do with a pair of jeans when she felt something crackling in the pocket. Thinking she better check before washing and bagging them, she stuck her hand in somewhat cautiously, not wanting to find anything grim. What she found was worse than she could have imagined. She plonked down on the bed, her heart beating so fast she started shaking. There must be a reason for this. She tried to remember when he'd last worn these jeans, but her mind couldn't focus. All she knew was that he didn't use condoms with her, so why were there two unopened packets in his jeans pocket? They hadn't done much together recently, but she'd put their distance down to his stress and work problems. Had he simply been relieving himself?

*Don't be stupid*, she thought to herself. *Surely there must be a sensible explanation.* She continued to sit and stare at the packets in her hands and couldn't move. Then she rapidly stuffed them back where she'd found them. Then, in turmoil, she retrieved them again. She thought back to the unnatural strain between them. She remembered the vague replies and his late return. She considered his aloofness. Oh no, surely not. He'd said he would never cheat. He'd told her that again, so recently. There must be another explanation.

Jen wasn't sure how long she sat there, shaking and disbelieving, trying hard to put a positive spin on this unwitting discovery. She sensed, rather than heard, Mike's keys in the door, his footsteps on the stairs and still she sat, immobile, with the loathsome facts in her hands. This was how he found her.

As he pushed open the bedroom door, still she sat unmoving. He glanced at her hands and froze in the doorway.

"What are these?" she asked.

"I think you can see that," he answered. She imagined him trying to think what to say. After a pause, he continued, "You obviously went through my pockets."

"I was doing no more than I have ever done in the past. I was clearing out and tidying up. I was going to wash your jeans before bagging them up," she said. "Last time, we were both pleased with my clear-out. Why have you got them?"

"Why do you think?"

"Tell me." She raised her voice in anguish. "Tell me! Who is it?"

"You don't need to know. Jen, I'm so, so sorry."

"Tell me," she whispered, tears springing to her eyes. "Is it Diana?"

He sank onto the bed beside her and put his head in his hands. "Yes," he murmured.

"Why? What have I done wrong, or not done?"

"I don't know. Nothing. She was there."

"I was here. You said just the other week that you'd never do this. We said we'd always be honest with each other. We made vows."

"Oh, Jen, I don't know why. I love you, I really do." He went to put his arm around her.

She stood quickly. "I can't do this now," she replied. "I need to be on my own."

"Do you want me to go?"

"Yes. No. I don't know. Go where? To her?"

"No, she's at home with Greg now."

"Oh no, poor Greg. Does he know?" She suddenly thought about kind, gentle, loving Greg.

"I don't think he knows. He doesn't need to know, Jen, unless you want to tell him. He doesn't need to be hurt too, does he?"

Jen was suddenly mad with anger. She kicked out at the bed. "You selfish, selfish sod! How could you do this? How could she? I thought she was my friend. You talk about loyalty to work colleagues. You talk about loyalty to team mates. You and your high ideals when it comes to all sorts of things. What happened to loyalty and trust with me? I'm your wife." Her voice rose with her anguish. "I want you to go. I don't care where. Just go. Get out and leave me alone."

She shouted with passion. Then she ran out of the bedroom and down the stairs. She entered the living room and slammed the door shut, flinging herself in a heap on the sofa. She clung to a cushion and heaved great gulping sobs of rejection, humiliation and loss.

After some time, she became aware of floorboards creaking above and realised that all had been quiet upstairs for a while. She stopped crying, frightened he would come to find her when all she wanted was to be alone. Then she heard his footsteps on the stairs. The living room door opened slowly. She sat up. Her eyes felt swollen and she knew they would be red and ugly. Mike just stood there, looking at her forlornly.

"I didn't think you'd ever find out," he said. "I didn't mean for it to be like this, to hurt you."

"Just go," she whispered, shaking her head.

"I'll be at Alex's," he said. "I rang him. He said I could go there for a while since he's on his own at the moment." He turned and left the room and Jen heard the front door close after him.

She sat up and, with tears still rolling down her face, she watched him walk along the front path to the gate. She saw him fling a bag in and then climb into his car. He sat for a moment without moving, head down. Then she heard the engine start and the car pulled away. In the back of her mind, she hoped he would drive safely. Then she wryly considered that, after everything, she was still concerned for his safety.

Unaware of how long she sat, clutching the cushion to her, Jen eventually got up and wandered aimlessly into the kitchen. Then she climbed the stairs and pushed open the bedroom door. The offending jeans had disappeared, as had all evidence of Mike's disloyalty and betrayal. She sagged down onto the bed, all impetus for action gone. She didn't know what to do. She thought of speaking to Pat but couldn't find the motivation to do even that. She just wanted to curl up and hide. Her mobile phone buzzed in her pocket. Retrieving it, she saw it was Mike calling. She couldn't bring herself to answer it. It stopped, but then a few minutes later it rang again. Sighing, she pressed the button to answer the call.

"I'm just calling to see if you are alright," Mike said.

"Oh yes, fine," Jen responded briefly and cut the call. She certainly couldn't speak to him at the moment. She was completely drained of all emotion and feeling not only rejection, but also betrayal and loneliness. She couldn't understand Diana's selfishness. She wondered what she had done to cause Mike's infidelity too. The more she thought about it, the more she felt she must be lacking appeal. She had never felt so rejected and useless.

How could one person treat another so horribly, especially one they professed to love?

# CHAPTER 16

When Jen arrived at school on Monday, several people asked if she was alright because she looked tired and pale. She had spoken to no-one during the rest of the weekend. She couldn't even bring herself to speak to Pat, because somehow it made it all so much more real to voice her distress and confusion. There had been no further calls from Mike either. She vaguely knew Alex, with whom he was apparently staying.

One of the hardest things that Jen had to do was enter the staffroom at lunchtime. She had avoided going in at playtime, but she knew she couldn't dodge going there forever. There was an informal meeting to discuss the Christmas concert arrangements, so she collected a cup of tea and quietly edged her way to a seat with her back to the window. The morning had been okay, although she was finding it difficult to get motivated. She was dog-tired. There had been moments, however, when her mind had been completely engaged with the children in her care, for which she was very grateful.

Sheila was reminding staff about dates for various events. The school post box would go out the following week, and she was asking for a volunteer to smarten it up after its annual bashing from the previous year, when the Year 6s had moved it daily to empty and distribute the contents. Concert tickets and other arrangements were discussed, as well as various other aspects of the season. Lastly, they talked about the more detailed organisation for Christmas lunches for children and the staff and governors' get-together at the end of term. Throughout all this, Jen was on autopilot and mumbled responses and opinions when required. At this point, she didn't feel in the Christmas spirit at all.

As conversation became desultory and the meeting finished, people began to mill about and leave the room. Sally came and sat in the empty seat next to Jen.

"Are you not feeling too good?"

"I had a bad night. I didn't sleep too well," Jen answered. "I'm feeling off colour today, that's all."

"Poor you. Well, if you sicken for something, please don't give it to me." Sally lowered her voice. "Between us, Christopher has asked me out to dinner on Saturday. I told him about that new place that's just opened up in Silver Street. My neighbour was raving about it, and I was telling him I'd love to try it."

"I don't think I'm sickening," said Jen. "I'm just shattered."

"Oh, well, let's hope that's all, of course," Sally smiled. "I'm really looking forward to being with Christopher again. He's so kind and gentle, and the way he cares for Charlie is just lovely."

"It's going alright then, your friendship?" Jen enquired.

"We get on really well, although he's quite busy, of course, so we can't get together that often."

"Are you making progress?"

"I'm sure we are, but it's hard when I have Mum to look after, and he has Charlie and his work. Changing the subject, I'm really looking forward to Christmas. The staff and governors' do should be fun this year, if we can bring partners. I shall ask Christopher, of course."

"Mmm," Jen muttered. At the moment, she could think of nothing she wished to avoid more. Then she tried to stop feeling sorry for herself. *Think about Pat*, she thought. *It must be worse for her, since she has the boys to consider, as well as the fact that it has all happened before.* Did that make it easier or worse? She wasn't sure. Then Jen realised that Sally had been speaking again, and she had missed what she had said. "Sorry, what was that? I was miles away."

"I was just saying that Christopher is so conscientious. He makes sure Charlie keeps in touch with his other grandparents as well as Christopher's own mum and dad. It must be hard. When he marries again, I'm not sure how his new wife will take to all that."

Jen wondered if Sally saw herself in that role. She still couldn't help thinking that it sounded as though Sally was more keen than Christopher and seemed to be doing more of the running.

Just then, the whistle blew in the distance and glancing at her watch, Jen gasped and they both hurried to the classrooms to retrieve their children.

That afternoon was a full rehearsal for the Christmas concert. Each class had been learning songs, but this would be the first time they had come together for a practice. The older children were mainly involved in singing and narrating, while the younger ones were performing the nativity story with hosts of angels and large flocks of sheep. These days, with all the demands of the national curriculum, there was not much time given over to rehearsing, but Graham Lockwood still believed that performing was good for children's confidence, and parents really loved to come and watch. They would do an afternoon performance just for grandparents and playgroups too. The Year 6 children would serve tea and cakes to the older folk after that one.

As the afternoon progressed, Jen lost herself in the activity. Charlie was supposed to play the innkeeper. Jen had been tempted to give him the part of Joseph. He would have charmed the audience, but he was still getting tired easily. As it turned out, this afternoon he took the part of the angel Gabriel, because the child who was meant to play him had been sent home poorly the day before. Charlie was so good that Jen decided to keep him in that part. He was confident and cheerful with the news he had to impart to Mary. His curly hair, which had grown back, shone like a halo and his round face was positively cherubic. By the end of the rehearsal, Jen realised her work had saved her day.

A few days later, after she had seen the children out at the end of the day, Jen turned to tidy her classroom. The lack of routine during the last session, when they had again practised for the concert, had led to unaccustomed disorder. By the time she had done all that, most staff had already left. She was in no hurry to get home. Her classroom cleaner had finished work, teachers weary from the slightly chaotic nature of the afternoon had left and the caretaker had checked all the windows and locked all the outside doors except the main entrance.

Jen was now reluctantly gathering her bags and bits. She knew there was only a chilly emptiness awaiting her at home, and so she was putting off leaving. She also knew she really should go and see Pat to tell her what had happened. It was just that she was feeling so totally useless that she wasn't sure she even had the energy to take that step.

Having got her things and put her coat on, Jen slumped down into her chair, suddenly feeling weary. Over the last few days, the same thoughts had gone round and round in her head like a nightmare carousel ride. How could a so-called 'friend' have deceived and betrayed her like that? They had gone to dinner at her flat, and Diana had appeared to be kindness itself.

Jen suddenly remembered the comment Diana had made to Mike about keeping fit and the teasing smile with which she had delivered the remark. Suddenly, it took on a whole new meaning, but they had all laughed at the time in what she'd thought was a companionable way. Jen started to shake again with renewed shock.

At that moment, there was a knock at the door and Charlie's dad came in.

"Sorry to bother you," Christopher said, and then he stopped abruptly. "Oh my goodness, are you alright? The front door was still open, and Jim said it would be okay to pop down."

"Yes, of course," said Jen, rousing herself and plastering a smile on her face. "How can I help?"

"Charlie left his lunchbox. My mum is visiting for the day, so she's with him and I thought I'd pop down and collect it before it starts festering."

"No problem," said Jen, dragging herself up to show him where it was.

"I'm really sorry to bother you. You've been so kind to us, and if there's anything I can help you with…"

"It's just something at home," Jen said evasively.

"I didn't mean to be nosey," Christopher said.

Jen, already feeling fragile, suddenly desperately needed to share her sadness. Tears of fatigue and despair came to her eyes. She stopped walking to the cloakroom. Turning and staring at the floor, she blurted out, "It's Mike, he's left. He's been seeing someone else. Sorry, sorry, I didn't mean to embarrass you."

"You haven't, not at all." After a second's hesitation, Christopher took a step towards her, extending his hand to touch her arm.

Having at last spoken the dreaded words, Jen simply couldn't stop the flood. "This is so embarrassing, I'm really sorry," she muttered.

"Please, don't feel awkward. I know what it's like to feel desperate, and sometimes you just need to voice it. I understand, I really do." His voice lowered.

Jen immediately felt even worse. Unwittingly he had shown her that her situation was not as desperate as his had been, and yet he wasn't making that point at all.

"Oh goodness," she said. "I'm so sorry for making a fuss."

"Look, we all need comfort in times of stress," he added, and instinctively, it seemed, he opened his arms and she took shelter there.

After a minute or two, they both quite naturally and unashamedly broke away and sat on the edge of a table in the classroom. There she told him everything. She opened up to him about whom it was that Mike had been seeing, and the double betrayal. He listened in silence, and she was thankful for the lack of meaningless platitudes and banal comments that he might have made. In his silence, he seemed to show that he recognised her distress. After a while, Jen's internal storm subsided and she smiled wryly.

"I'm really sorry. I think you caught me at the wrong moment," she said, looking straight into his green eyes.

"Or at the right moment," he said. "Sometimes a sounding board can help."

"You've certainly helped me. Thank you. I suppose we better go. Your mum will be wondering where you are, and Jim will be waiting to lock up."

They found the lunchbox. Jen gathered her things and they headed up the corridor to the front door. They met Jim as they went, and Jen was grateful that he hadn't come upon them in the classroom. He might have got the wrong end of the stick and made the wrong assumptions about their relationship.

They said goodnight to him and left the building. In the car park, Jen apologised again.

"Please, I hope we count as friends," Christopher said. "What is this world if we can't help our friends? I'm sure I've heard you say something like that."

On her way home, Jen reflected on her outburst. She thought she should feel embarrassed, but she didn't. With the release of emotion, she realised she was ready to go and see Pat. Parking up outside her friend's house, she checked her watch. The boys would have had their tea by now, and Pat would be able to chat before bath time.

When Pat answered the door, she showed mild surprise. It was rare for Jen to call at this time of day. "Come in, come in," Pat welcomed. "It seems ages since we chatted properly."

Jen was aware of Pat looking at her closely, but without saying more her friend turned and she followed Pat down the hallway and past the living room.

"So, what's up?" asked Pat as Jen followed her into the kitchen.

Jen took a deep breath, and with her voice carefully under control she dropped the bombshell. Pat turned from filling the kettle and just looked at her. Without a word, she put the kettle down and gave Jen a hug. Then, rummaging up her sleeve for a tissue, Jen sat down and Pat sat opposite.

"Tell me," she said simply and quietly.

Having already opened up to Christopher, Jen found it easier to tell her friend everything. Pat was shocked, Jen could see, not least because it was Diana that Mike had been seeing. She'd had no idea.

"I wonder if being with Doug so much gave him ideas," she said after listening for some time.

"I just feel as if I've let him down somehow. As for her, I don't think I'll ever forgive her. It's all the lies and cheating and sneaking around. I imagine they had a good old laugh at my expense, feeling they'd made plans and got away with it. I feel so humiliated."

"I'm the last person to give advice, aren't I?" Pat smiled ruefully.

"Oh, Pat, what a pair we are."

One thing Jen had decided not to share with Pat was her breaking down in front of Christopher, and the fact that he had held her and comforted her. She couldn't analyse why she didn't want to share that. After all, there was nothing to it. Christopher was becoming Sally's partner, and to her he was no more than an acquaintance. Pat might get the wrong idea.

"How are you?" Jen asked.

"I'm plodding along. There are good days and bad days. The boys see Doug quite regularly." She dropped her voice. "They think he's on a course. Did I tell you that before? I'm sure they believe it. It's early days yet, but we're getting into a sort of routine. He's saying sorry all the time and making noises about coming back. He says it definitely won't happen again and that he loves us."

"Would you have him back? I know you said it's not the first time."

"I'm holding out at the moment. It's too soon to decide. I haven't rationalised to myself all the humiliation and rejection yet. He can think for a bit longer, and I need more time," replied Pat.

"All I can say is that now I understand. Thank you for everything," said Jen. "I better be going, then you can sort the boys out for bed."

Back at Jen's house, the heating had come on but it still seemed empty and cold. She had just put down her things when the doorbell rang. She hurriedly slipped out of her coat and reached for the latch. She hoped it wasn't Mike; she couldn't cope with any more this evening.

When she opened the door, she was surprised and not too happy to see who was there. "Hello, come in, Greg," she said, opening the door wider.

Greg followed her down the hall to the living room. "Do you want a glass of wine or a cup of tea or coffee?"

"I'd love a whisky, but I'll settle for a cup of tea," said Greg.

Jen went into the kitchen, and after a moment he followed. She turned, and as he came in he scooped her into his arms. He was very tall, and she only came up to his chest. They stood without speaking for several moments. Then he finally released her.

"Jen, I'm so sorry."

"Greg, it's not your fault! I imagine you are feeling as bad as me. How did you find out?"

"She told me. She just came out with it. She said she'd rather I heard it from her than from anyone else." Then he quietly added, "It's not the first time, you see. It's why we've never married. I didn't feel secure enough for that, but I love her. She says she thinks it will probably be over — now that we all know. I certainly didn't see it coming, though."

"She says it's over? Just like that?" asked Jen disbelievingly. "She's caused absolute devastation and she can just walk away as if it didn't matter?"

"It takes two to tango, you know, Jen," Greg responded quietly.

"Yes, of course," she said.

He took her in his arms again and kissed the top of her head. "Why couldn't I have met you first?"

"What a mess," Jen whispered into his chest. After a few moments, she broke free to make the tea. "What will you do?" she asked.

"I don't know, probably nothing."

They went through to the living room and Jen sank into the sofa. She just wanted to close her eyes and hide from everything and everyone. She felt Greg's eyes upon her. She imagined she was showing how exhausted she was.

"I'll always be here for you, Jen," Greg said.

Jen smiled wanly. "I know, Greg, thank you."

He placed his half empty mug on the table and rose to leave, recognising that she needed to be on her own. "Please call me, whenever you need to," he said as he left.

Jen didn't get up. She didn't have the energy. She heard the front door close and Greg's footsteps fading away as he walked up the path.

# CHAPTER 17

Jen was so drained and worn out that she slept soundly that night, for which she was grateful. The new day dawned grey and windy and as she was on playground duty later, she dressed warmly. She couldn't bring herself to eat breakfast, but she grabbed a yoghurt pot, a packet of crisps and a couple of bits of fruit from the bowl just before she left the house.

During the previous evening, she had made a conscious effort to pull herself together. She wasn't the first person this had happened to, and she was going to cope and get back on track. She had a job she loved and a good home, for the time being, anyway. She was luckier than many.

On arriving at school, she got out of her car and headed for the front door at the same time as Lesley.

"Are you feeling better?" asked this half of the gruesome twosome, as Mike had christened her and Mary.

"Yes, I am," Jen responded. "Thank you for asking."

Lesley gave her a beaming smile. "Oh, good!"

Jen was quite amazed and wondered why she was being treated to such cordiality.

The morning proceeded much as any other. The children were starting to get tired, evidenced by the odd squabble and a little more noise than was usual. Lunchtime came and Jen headed for the staffroom. On this day each week, there was an informal meeting. It was not compulsory, but most staff turned up unless they had to nip out for something. It usually only lasted for fifteen or twenty minutes. Jen collected her lunch and a drink and, sitting, she stifled a large yawn. The first item of information caused quite a stir.

Mary had decided to leave and take early retirement. "I shan't be going until the summer," she announced. "This should give Mr Lockwood plenty of time to find a replacement. Then we shan't have to have a temporary teacher. Hopefully that will be better for everyone."

Jen smiled internally but managed to keep a straight face. She imagined others would be feeling the same, and Sally caught her eye from across the room. So this was why Lesley had been so polite and even friendly as she had arrived that morning. If Mary was going, she would be losing her ally and so would be feeling vulnerable.

As she and Sally walked back along the corridor to their classrooms after lunch, there was only one topic of conversation.

"Well, she's finally going," Sally said. "I know the parents like her and she gets good results from the children, but she can be so awful in the staffroom."

"I shan't be sorry to see her go, I admit," agreed Jen. "I feel as if I've had my share of her spite recently."

"I imagine not getting this promotion recently gave her food for thought," Sally added.

"I suppose it must be hard, after all her time at this school, to see someone like me swoop in under her nose and take it," Jen sighed.

"You got it because you deserve it," Sally said with conviction.

"Thanks, I need that sort of support. Things are a bit tricky at home at the moment, between you and me, but I'm looking forward to taking on the new role."

"Sorry to hear that," Sally said sympathetically.

By the end of the week, Jen was thoroughly glad to have a

break. She had kept her brave face on at work and colleagues had not discovered the real reasons for her tiredness and lack of bounce.

Mike telephoned her on Saturday morning. She hadn't been up long. Although she had woken early, she had determinedly stayed in bed.

"Hello," Jen said once she'd picked up the phone.

"Jen, how are you?"

"I'm fine," she answered automatically. "Well, you know," she added.

"We need to talk. Can we talk?"

"Maybe in a few days," said Jen with caution. "I need space and thinking time."

"Of course," Mike said. "I understand. Jen, I'm really, really sorry. I think it's over now, anyway."

"Mike, I'm not doing this over the phone," she said with determination.

"No, no, you're right, sorry. Diana asked me to say she's sorry too."

*Oh well, that's alright then*, Jen thought. She didn't know what to say to that, so she said nothing. There was a long pause.

Then Mike said, "Jen, she wants to meet you. She wants to apologise."

"No, no way!" said Jen, her voice rising. "Sorry doesn't even come close. There's no way I want to speak to her at the moment, especially just to make her feel better. Mike, I have to go. Call me towards the end of next week. Maybe we'll talk then. Bye," she added hastily, before he could argue.

"Okay, but I'm so very sorry, Jen. Go carefully. I love you. Bye."

*Yeah right*, Jen thought as she cut the call. She paced around the kitchen, both hurt and angry.

Sorry really didn't fix anything. As for love, he didn't know the meaning of the word. She kicked a chair.

Last year at her previous school, she had gone on a course to learn about the stages of loss or grief that a child might experience when a parent or sibling dies or divorce is happening around them. She reflected on this now. She reckoned she must be moving from the denial and isolation stage to that of anger. The first stage had shielded her from the immediate shock and wave of pain. Initially she had found it really hard to tell Pat, and all she wanted to do was hide away.

Now she felt *so* angry. She mooched about the house for quite some time, swearing and talking to herself.

The following week were the Christmas concert performances, and, on the Monday, it was the dress rehearsal-cum-performance for the playgroups and older community. Jen had spent the rest of her time over the weekend baking dozens of fairy cakes and biscuits for the tea party afterwards. It had been a good activity to keep her occupied. She had battered and mixed and then cooked and designed toppings. She had piled them onto trays and carefully conveyed them to school on the back seat of her car. She and Sally had decided to keep the children very busy during the morning with more formal learning activities, so that they were kept out of mischief and didn't get too excited prior to their concert.

After lunch, once all the children had been to the toilet, a necessary precaution at their age, Jen gave the children a pep talk about leaving their clothes in tidy piles. She remembered her newly qualified teacher year when she had omitted this stage of the programming and had returned from the play that year to find children with odd socks and wearing someone else's jumper at home time. It had taken ages to sort out, since not all parents labelled clothing.

Several parent helpers had come in and began to get the children ready. Jen had placed the children's costumes on the tables, so it was all very calm and organised. True to tradition, there were the normal incidents of the youngest children taking off *all* their clothes, presumably forgetting what they were doing and thinking they were getting ready for bed. It had happened several times before prior to PE lessons, so no-one laughed. Then one child got both feet down the same trouser leg and tumbled over. Tears were quickly mopped up, and one of the parents sorted her out. Eventually everyone was ready and sitting on the carpet, waiting for their call.

A couple of stripy shepherds' cloths slipped off heads and clips were found to secure them. The host of angels didn't have wings because they would have been too much of a liability, but they looked enchanting in their white, floaty costumes and silver sparkly haloes. Joseph and Mary were ready and waiting nervously with the innkeeper, and Charlie, as the Angel Gabriel, was sitting right in front of Jen, stroking her foot. Several children of this age did that. She didn't mind. He was quiet but seemed happy and smiled up at her when she caught his eye. She smiled back at him and gave him a wink.

Then the message came and Jen got her children ready to go into the hall. It was so hard for them to be quiet, but the older children were singing a carol and so she got her class to hum the tune quietly so that they weren't chattering and spoiling the atmosphere. They entered the hall on cue and took their places. There were several 'aahs' from the older folk and one or two children waved to their grandparents. This performance was always a little noisy since the playgroups were in to watch, but it was a good chance for them to visit the 'big' school.

Jen had been finding it very difficult to feel like celebrating, but even with all her present tensions she took delight in the earnestness of the little ones, who were trying so hard to do their best and remember their words.

When they had finished and the older children had sung their last carol, Graham came to the stage and gave thanks to everyone. He invited the grandparents and other older folk to stay for refreshments and congratulated the children on their hard work.

Their next performance was the following evening and would be for parents, so everyone had time to pick up and correct the little errors that had occurred. However, the audience all seemed to have enjoyed it, and there were several comments to Jen as she left the hall with her class. One lady grasped her hand and thanked her profusely for restoring her faith in the community, which had been severely shaken after her house was broken into recently. Jen was touched and smiled into the misty blue eyes of the old lady.

The following evening, Jen had to be back in school before six o'clock. It hardly seemed worth going home, so she stayed and ate some of her unfinished lunch in the staffroom.

She wondered what Mike was doing and with whom. He had suggested his affair was over, but Jen was feeling insecure and vulnerable. Fortunately, she didn't have long to think like this, as other staff and children soon started reappearing. There were always some who came really early because parents wanted a front-row seat. With a deep breath, Jen rose and went down the corridor to her classroom. The same process as yesterday afternoon started, and following a few last-minute costume fixes they were all trooping to the hall again.

As Jen took her place at the side of the stage with her group of youngsters, she had a moment to scan the hall. She saw several of her children's parents, and in the second row she saw Christopher Mayhew. When Charlie came onto the stage, she was struck by the expression on his father's face. He was more than proud — he looked jubilant, joyous. Jen guessed it was Christopher's mum sitting next to him. There was something of a family resemblance, and she saw the older lady whisper something.

She was proved correct when, at the end of the performance, this same lady came to the classroom to collect Charlie. She asked if it would be alright if Charlie showed her around the class. Jen was only too pleased. She stayed with them for a few minutes and then explained that she needed to take the last of the children to another class to meet an older brother.

Jen was just returning when, walking through the hall, she saw Sally and Christopher at the far door. They were clearly having an in-depth conversation, and Sally didn't look too happy. Jen saw her raise both hands in the air and grasp Christopher's arm. Jen thought the expression on Sally's face looked pleading. She didn't linger. There was no-one else about.

Most people had collected their children and left, and the few who were still milling about were closer to the front entrance by now. Jen hurried back to her classroom just as Charlie and his Granny were leaving too.

"Thank you so much," said Mrs Mayhew. She gave Jen a sincere smile. "You must be Mrs Lucas. Jen, did Christopher say your name was? He was saying how very supportive and compassionate you've been. We both owe you our warmest gratitude."

"Please, there's no need," answered Jen. "I wanted to be useful."

"More than that," she responded. "Anyway, 'thank you' seems feeble for how we feel about what you did." She patted Jen's shoulder. "I feel sure we shall meet again," she added as she moved past Jen.

Charlie gave her a little wave.

After they had all left and she was on her own, Jen had time for reflection. She thought of the encounter she had witnessed between Sally and Christopher. She was suddenly overcome with envy — or was it jealousy? Did she want a relationship with Christopher, as Sally appeared to have? Ridiculous! What was that all about? She mentally chastised herself. She was lonely, and her life was complicated. She hurriedly collected her things.

# CHAPTER 18

The next morning, both children and staff were tired. At the end of the previous week, Sally and Jen had planned a day for the children that would take this into account, but it was still quite hard work to keep the classes on track.

Jen had not slept well, having such a lot going round in her head. It seemed that Sally was feeling out of sorts too. Jen heard her raising her voice during the morning, which was something that never normally happened. Just before playtime, Jen spoke to her teaching assistant.

"Jodie, would you do me a big favour? Would you fetch me a cup of tea when the children go outside so that I can have it here? I've got a cracking headache," she fibbed.

"Of course," Jodie responded straight away. "Have you got any paracetamol?"

"Yes, that's fine, thanks," Jen said. She just couldn't face the staffroom this morning.

"I'll just pop next door and ask Sally if she wants one, if that's okay with you," Jodie suggested. "She seemed a bit down this morning too."

Jen nodded at her and started to organise the children into packing away their things and getting their coats on for playtime. Just as they were leaving the classroom, Jodie reappeared with two mugs of tea and a plate of biscuits.

"You're a star," said Jen, heaving a great sigh.

"No problem, I'll just take this next door. Do you want me to stay and help set up for the next session?"

"No, that's alright. I'm going to sit them down and have a few minutes of quiet time after play, so you could do it then," said Jen. "You go on up to the staffroom and grab a rest. You've certainly earned it this morning."

After she had gone, Sally appeared.

"Hi. Do you mind if I come and sit for a couple of minutes?"

Jen imagined it might be more than two minutes, and she had some idea of what might follow.

"Christopher and I had a few words last night," Sally began. "Well, not words exactly, but I think he's backing off."

"Oh, I'm sorry," said Jen and she meant it. Sally really wanted this relationship. Perhaps that was the trouble. "Maybe it all needs to be a bit more casual. This is his first expedition back into the dating arena since his wife died. He's probably nervous."

"Maybe I've been a bit too keen," Sally said, echoing Jen's thoughts. "But he's such a lovely guy, and I'm sure we could build something good together."

They chatted for a few minutes longer. Whoever was outside on playground duty must have decided to give the children, and staff, a bit longer than the normal fifteen minutes today. There was watery sunshine, and although it was cold Jen imagined everyone would benefit.

"Thanks for listening and for the advice," said Sally. "I better get cracking; they'll be back in any minute now. And I'll try and back off a bit with Christopher."

That evening was the last of the Christmas concert performances. All was going according to plan when, just as the children were being called to the hall, there was an urgent telephone call for Sally.

"You go and take it," Jen said. "The teaching assistants and I can cope. All the children know what they're doing."

Sally hurried off to the office and Jen could see the worried expression on her face. It was unusual to have an important call at this time. She knew that Sally would immediately think of her mother at home by herself, finding it difficult to do anything unassisted these days.

The concert started and all was going well. The children were really trying so hard to get everything right. Jen noticed the empty chair where Sally had sat for the previous two performances and she wondered what was amiss.

After all was done and Mr Lockwood had said his piece, again the children filed out to their classrooms to get dressed. Parents soon joined them and there was a lot of milling about. As parents and children disappeared home, Christopher approached Jen.

"Thank you so much for giving Charlie the confidence to do all that," he said. "He's really flourished in your care since his accident. I'm glad his hair has grown back." He chuckled. "A bald Angel Gabriel wouldn't have had the same effect."

Jen smiled her agreement and nodded. "He has done really well," she said.

"I gather Sally's mum has taken a turn for the worse," he said. "Sheila was just telling me when I asked her if she knew where Sally was."

"Oh dear," said Jen. "I wondered if that was the problem. There was a phone call and she didn't reappear."

"I wanted to have a word with her, but it'll have to wait. She won't want me bothering her right now."

"I'm sure she wouldn't mind," Jen considered. "She thinks a lot of you."

"We've had some pleasant times together recently, but I'm not looking for anything more yet with Sally," he said candidly. "I don't want to give her the wrong impression by pestering her when she's anxious about her mum. On the other hand, I don't want her to think I'm ignoring her." He frowned. "Sorry, I'm pestering you now with my worries." He smiled. "I seem to be relying on your good sense yet again."

"You might call and ask after her mum," Jen suggested. "It would be odd not to; after all, you're good friends. If Sally wants to go out again, you could always say that you're not in a position to go out too much at the moment, but you may find she's alright with that. I'm sure she knows you both have complicated commitments." She was wary of interfering or giving bad advice, but she didn't want to just sit on the fence either.

"Are you feeling any better?" Christopher asked her.

Jen was still feeling a bit awkward about having broken down in front of him during their previous encounter. "I'm jogging along," she replied. "Mike and I have some sorting out to do. He wanted to meet and talk, but I asked him to ring me after these performances were out of the way. I suppose we'll do that this weekend."

"Life is complicated sometimes," Christopher said. "Ultimately, you have to do what feels right for you, because if you don't it will be wrong for both of you. That's what I believe, anyway."

"I suppose so," Jen answered, not really knowing what was right for her at this point.

"I must get Charlie home. Come on, Charlie," he called to his son, who was engrossed in playing with the Lego that Jen had put out earlier.

"See you both in the morning," Jen said, smiling as Christopher helped Charlie put the bricks away.

# CHAPTER 19

As Jen was anticipating, there was a call from Mike early on Saturday morning.

"Hello," she answered cautiously. She was still in bed.

"Can we meet? Please."

Jen was not looking forward to this at all. "You better come round," she said.

"To the house?"

"Yes." It was all a bit stilted.

"Okay, good. When shall I come?"

"Aren't you at the gym this morning?" Jen asked.

"Well, I would be normally," he said. "But I'd rather come and see you. I want to explain."

Jen felt it might take quite a lot of explaining, but she said, "Come about eleven, then, and we'll talk."

"I'll see you later, Jen," Mike said. "I love you."

She wished he wouldn't keep saying that. He wasn't usually demonstrative. "See you at eleven," was all she managed in return.

Having finished the call, Jen felt restless so she got up, straightened the bedroom, had a shower and got dressed. She was tired and, feeling cross and rebellious, she really didn't want to make too much effort with her appearance. She pulled on her jeans and found a jumper. She blow-dried her hair and found some earrings that matched her top. She only applied mascara and a minimal amount of lip gloss. That would have to do. In order to keep busy, she gave the bathroom and kitchen a good clean.

Just before eleven, there was a knock at the door. Jen peeled off her rubber gloves and went to the front door. Mike had kept his keys as far as she knew, so it was sensitive of him to knock, she supposed grudgingly. She could see his outline in the central glass panel and took a deep breath before opening the door.

She paused before inviting him in. Mike was there, holding some flowers and looking remorseful. Jen didn't say anything. She didn't know what to say. She stood to one side, and he came past her and headed for the kitchen. He turned to her, holding out the flowers as she came in behind him.

"Thank you," she said, taking them and looking in the cupboard for a vase. "They smell lovely," she added, burying her nose in the bouquet. Anything to mask the awkwardness of the moment.

"Jen…" Mike started.

"Wait," she said. "Give me a moment. Let me do these first. You could put the kettle on."

Jen, having arranged the flowers and Mike having made a cup of tea for each of them, went into the living room together. Sitting on separate sofas, they looked at each other.

"You better go first," Jen said, looking down at her white-knuckled hands in her lap.

"Now I'm here, I don't know what to say, where to start," Mike said, hanging his head. Then, after a moment, he blurted, "I'm so, so sorry."

"When did it start? Were you seeing her when we went for dinner that last time?" Jen asked dispassionately.

Mike lifted his head and looked her in the eye. "Yes. I'm going to be absolutely honest with you, Jen, and I'll try to answer any questions."

Tears seeped into Jen's eyes. "Why?" she whispered. "What was I not giving you?"

"I don't know. Really, I don't know. You were giving me everything."

"Yes, I thought I was," Jen answered with force. "I've been trying really hard to be understanding of your work, your mood." She was conscious of her voice rising but felt unable not to show her anger. "I was bending over backwards to be understanding."

"You were so wrapped up in your work. You're so successful and enjoying it so much," Mike responded with vigour. Then, with more restraint, he said, "Maybe I was jealous of that."

"Oh, Mike, if that was the case, I'm really sorry but I've always *felt* you came first, always," Jen said.

She sat quietly for several moments, thinking. Again she went over it in her mind and asked the questions she had demanded of herself before. Had she neglected him for her work? Had she shown too much interest in the people there at the expense of her husband? She remembered other peoples' responses to these questions — when she had spoken with Pat, for instance. She genuinely didn't think she had thought more of her work and ignored Mike. She sighed.

"Why with Diana? I thought she was my friend. How could she have been so disloyal, so treacherous, lying and cheating?" This came out fervently too.

"She's been unhappy at home. I felt sorry for her being bored with Greg and feeling stifled. She was there, lively and teasing. I fell for it. Jen, I wish it hadn't happened. Now, I feel like I went outside when everything was going right inside. I've ruined a good thing. I know that, but *please* give me another chance. I won't let you down again."

"I feel so humiliated," Jen murmured, tucking in her legs and curling up.

Mike slid off his seat, fell to his knees in front of her and took both her hands in his. "Don't, please don't." He cried out and his eyes became moist. "It's me, not you who should feel that, because I've been such an idiot."

They stayed in that tableau for what seemed like several minutes, neither knowing what to say or do next. In the end, Mike rose and sat on the sofa next to her. He hesitated, unsure of her, and then he put his arm around her shoulder. Automatically she leaned into him for comfort. The tears now slid silently down her face as she wept out all the damage and anxiety that she had held in check for so long.

"If you come back," she said, "I can't do this again, and I don't know if it'll work out or not."

"It's over," Mike said. "I won't do it again. It's you I love, really."

They stayed like that for some time. The flow of Jen's tears eventually stemmed, and she dug in her pocket for a tissue. Sitting up to blow her nose, she then stood.

"I'm going to the bathroom," she said and ran upstairs to wash her face and calm her nerves.

Could she do this, take him back? Somehow she knew she was going to, but would things ever be the same? She doubted it. She'd had that very thought about Pat and Doug when her friend had been having this dilemma recently. Jen thought about the vows she had made; for better, for worse and all that. She knew she would try to understand, accept some of the blame and try to forgive, even if she couldn't forget. Not for a while, anyway. Maybe in time, with work on both sides, she would learn to feel better about herself and gain confidence.

Slowly she returned downstairs. On re-entering the living room, she saw Mike with his back to her, hands in his pockets as he looked out of the window.

"You better go and get your things," she said.

He turned. "Oh, Jen, thank you," he said with a sigh and stepped towards her. She folded her arms, subconsciously protecting herself by retreating. He seemed to respect this and stepped away.

"I'll be back as soon as possible."

"Okay." She nodded and smiled wanly. She hoped this was the right decision.

While he was gone, Jen desperately wanted to call Pat. Perhaps she needed reassurance that this was the correct thing to be doing, or maybe she just craved a friendly voice to soothe her troubled spirit. She went to the kitchen to retrieve her phone from the worktop where she had left it.

When Pat answered, she asked, "Are you free for a quick chat?"

"Yes, fine," Pat answered.

"I haven't got long, but Mike has just been round. I just needed to talk to someone. It's not the sort of thing I can talk to Mum about. I haven't even told her Mike left. Last time she called, I just said he was out."

"Oh, Jen, she would be supportive, you know. Won't you have to tell her eventually, or are you hoping things will work out and you won't need to?"

"I know she would be there for me, but I wasn't sure how things would be and so I didn't want her to worry unnecessarily. Anyway, I felt so bad, as if I'd failed miserably and I just couldn't bring myself to confess that."

"Jen, no. It's not your failure," Pat responded with force. "So what did Mike come round for?"

"He says it's over with her, Diana, and he wants to come back. He says he's really sorry."

Jen paused as the thought passed around in her mind that Pat must have been through all this herself. She imagined that Pat could well be rolling her eyes, since Doug must have voiced similar things in the past, and here they were back to square one with Doug camping out at a friend's house. Jen persuaded herself that this was different.

She continued, "He says he won't let me down again. He was virtually crying."

"Have you given him an answer?"

"He's gone to collect his stuff and then he's coming home. I don't know if it's the right thing to be doing or not, but there we are..." Jen tailed off.

"We're all allowed to make a mistake, I guess. It won't be easy for you. I think you'll have to bite your tongue a lot and not use his affair as a weapon at any point, even if you're having an argument in the future. Also, you'll be wondering what he's doing every time he goes out. That's the hardest thing. That may last a while," Pat said.

"I feel like I'm swallowing a lot of pride. I feel very humiliated by this whole thing, but I suppose I've been to blame too."

"Well, I don't know about that, but one of you has to be prepared to give a lot and he has to be prepared to be reassuring too," said Pat.

"I know it's not going to be easy at first, but we used to have such a great relationship. I really feel I should make it work. After all, we both made promises when we married. I know he's not kept his, but I think I should try. We used to have such fun together. We've been good friends." She paused and then added, "Thanks for listening. I better go, he'll be back soon."

"Let me know how you go, and remember I'm always here if you need anything at any time," said Pat.

"I'll let you know. I really better go. I don't want to be caught discussing all this just yet. Thanks. Speak soon," Jen answered. "Bye."

She put her phone down and went back up to the bathroom to check on the state of her face and hair. She was determined to make an effort now. If she was going to do this, she would have to do it well.

The first week of being back together was a strain on both of them. Mike was trying hard, too hard, and Jen was trying to respond but finding it difficult. By some unspoken agreement, they slept in the same bed but that was all. In the mornings before work, Mike got up first and made Jen's breakfast. For him to do so every morning was unusual and so didn't seem natural. She was polite but couldn't bring herself to be warm. She was trying to be spontaneous but was feeling numbed. Each morning on her way to school, she was wondering if things would ever improve and each evening as she travelled home, she was dreading Mike being late and having to worry about why. However, to be fair, she thought, by the end of that week he had been very prompt and often in before her.

On the Saturday morning, she woke early.

When he finally stirred, she asked, "Are you going to the gym this morning? You didn't go last week."

"I'll not go if you want me to stay here," Mike replied.

"No, that would be daft. You can't stay chained to the house and me," Jen said.

"I'm not going to do anything I shouldn't. It's you I love. I shan't be seeing her again."

"I know. You said. I have to learn to trust you, that's all."

"Well, I'll go, but I shan't be out long."

"Stay as long as you need to," Jen said as stalwartly as she could.

They got up and a normal Saturday resumed.

True to his word, Mike was not gone very long and his kit was dirty, proving he had been where he said. He returned with flowers.

"They're lovely, thank you," said Jen as she took them into the kitchen. "You don't need to do this, though, Mike, although I do love them. It's not normal. We have to try and be normal."

"I just want to show you that I do care and I'm sorry."

"I know," she answered.

# CHAPTER 20

Christmas at school was completed, and Jen finished the term feeling pleased to have a break. She had been putting a brave face on things and trying to get into the spirit of all the celebrations with the children. She had deliberated over whether to go with the rest of the staff for their meal out. It was a tradition that included the caretaker, the cleaning staff, the teaching staff, the kitchen helpers, the dining room team and the headteacher. She had liked the idea at the beginning of term but now, despite her best intentions, she was wondering what Mike would do all evening while she was out. She squashed these thoughts down determinedly. Since she had let him come back, she would have to trust his word, or there was no point trying to make their marriage work.

Jen had dressed up and gone, staying out as long as the others although there was a great temptation to make excuses and go home early. Mike was at home when she returned. He was unshaven and lying on the sofa with a coffee and a magazine. He clearly hadn't been anywhere, and she had to believe he had not used his phone either.

The school holidays progressed. Mike went to work and came back as normal. Jen tried to chill out and catch up with household things. One time, he came home with a bottle of wine and a takeaway. They had a really pleasant evening and as Jen cleared up the dishes, Mike came up behind her, put his arms around her waist and kissed the back of her neck. That was all. He reached for the tea towel and the moment passed. Jen had felt relaxed about it and had actually enjoyed the moment of intimacy.

Before she knew it, Christmas was upon them. For the last couple of years they'd woken early and exchanged their main gifts in bed, normally followed by a bit of lazy lovemaking. Having had lunch together, they usually went to Jen's parents' house for their evening meal. Mike's parents lived abroad so it was a good, cosy arrangement and Jen's mum, Cath, always said Christmas wasn't Christmas without seeing family, so it kept her happy too.

This year, the practical arrangements were the same. Jen's family knew nothing of her recent distress. She had bought all her gifts and wrapped them, stowing them in the drawer under her side of the bed as usual. She guessed Mike had done the same. This time she felt a mix of excitement — born from years and years of enthusiasm for the season — but also a measure of anxiety about how things would pan out now.

Christmas morning dawned. Recently it had been consistently grey and dank with scudding clouds and bitter winds. This morning was cold and clear with the sun already trying to push through. Perhaps this was an omen, Jen thought, but then she immediately chided herself for being too superstitious and melodramatic. She would try and get back to making her own good fortune by being positive and decisive. With that thought, she kissed Mike's shoulder as he lay sleeping beside her. This was going to be a good Christmas; she had to make it so. They had been excellent friends until recently, and surely everyone deserved another chance. She knew that this special morning would be pivotal. He stirred awake and turned. As he did, she leaned in and kissed him again, this time on his lips, sending him a clear message.

"Happy Christmas," she murmured shyly.

"And back to you," he responded warmly with the ghost of a hesitant smile.

"Okay, now presents?" Jen asked, trying to sound cheerful and enthusiastic without overdoing it.

"Definitely," answered Mike. "It took me a long time to decide, so I do hope you like it." He stretched down his side of the bed, slid the drawer open and pulled out a package.

Jen reached for her gift at the same time, and as they met in the centre of the bed they both exclaimed, "Oh, hey!" and "Wow!" followed by genuine mirth.

They had both chosen the same wrapping. Jen had used silver ribbon and Mike had chosen gold, but the paper was identical.

"What are the chances?" he said, smiling at her, his eyes crinkling at the corners attractively.

They each unwrapped their presents. Jen held up a beautiful leather bag which she had admired from afar, until it was no longer in the shop to be coveted. Mike unwrapped the new sports clothing she knew he was after.

"It's beautiful," she said. "I've been looking at this for quite some time. I didn't think I could ever afford it, though. How did you know?"

"I debated with myself for ages, and then I double-checked with Pat exactly which one you liked," Mike said.

"My present to you is quite dull compared to this," Jen said.

"It definitely is not," Mike said forcefully. "It's the make and style I've really wanted. You know that. Will you be able to make use of the bag?"

"I will," she said. "I will." She murmured the words again to herself as she was reminded of the vows she'd made all those years ago.

Mike put his gifts down on the floor beside the bed and as he leaned back, he turned and put his arm across her. "Can I?" he asked.

"Yes," Jen replied, trying hard not to show the hesitancy she was feeling.

His hand crept under the covers in the familiar way. She remembered how she enjoyed this and she couldn't help but breathe out and begin to relax. Was this purely a physical thing, or was she rekindling her love for him? She wasn't sure, but at this moment she was enjoying the attention. After initial tentativeness, Mike took the lead in their lovemaking, being both tender and respectful.

Tears oozed out of Jen's eyes and poured down her cheeks. She tried to hide her face by snuggling into him, but Mike eventually felt the wetness on his neck and asked her worriedly if he had hurt her. How could she explain when she hardly knew herself? Of course she was hurting, but not in the way he meant. She was trying to quash unwelcome questions. Was she better at it than Diana? Did they say the same things to each other? Did he cry her name when he came? Had he been picturing her as they made love here and now?

"No, you didn't hurt me," Jen said eventually when she had some command over her voice. After a few moments, she added, "I'm sorry."

"No, it's me who's sorry," Mike responded.

The rest of Christmas Day and the few days following were calm and generally restful. Mike seemed to be cruising along happily, almost as if nothing had happened. Jen felt it was as if he thought now that it was over between Diana and him, everything could be completely back to normal.

She remembered some trite words from a magazine she had been idly reading in the dentist's waiting room: a relationship without trust is like a car without fuel. You can stay in it as long as you like, but it won't go anywhere.

She tried really hard not to show him that she was wondering what he was up to every time he left the house. To be fair, Mike was not staying out late or going to the gym too much. He was home from work in good time and he did as much round the house as he used to do. He was attentive to Jen and their lovemaking was progressing.

So why was she this uneasy?

# CHAPTER 21

In the New Year, Jen took up her increased responsibility with home/school liaison as well as continuing with her classroom role. She was extremely busy during school hours, planning and implementing, and time passed rapidly. She had tried very hard to keep school away from home and only worked at the weekend when Mike was at the gym. January and February were cold and generally wet, but as they slipped into March there were signs of the weather improving again.

As part of her new job, she had visited some of the families who had agreed to receive extra support. Mrs Jones had consented to use a positive behaviour chart at home with Johnny, and together they had identified the things that would help the most. One of these was a regular, earlier bedtime and both mother and son had agreed the rewards for success. Jen had also visited another parent to discuss her son's bedwetting problem, because it was causing concerns in school with the lad being called names, since he was not always smelling hygienic. Jen was able to suggest some strategies but also said that a visit to the doctor might help too.

Since Christopher Mayhew was a single parent, Jen had also visited him. He had asked to be included in the project because he was concerned that his young son might be missing out on something that he, as a parent, should be doing. This was not such a sensitive visit and was probably unnecessary. Jen was happy to be going just to ensure that there was nothing delicate that Christopher wanted to discuss with her away from the school setting. Sometimes, in her experience, this did happen and a parent might disclose something important that would help a child in school. After all, every parent could be influenced by their own experiences of school, whether good or bad.

Christopher was welcoming, and this time he had tidied the house and prepared a tray with coffee and biscuits. "Last time you came, I was very lacking in hospitality," he said.

"Not at all." Jen laughed. "You had far more on your plate than offering us a hot drink. As I said then, it was great to see you and Charlie at home and so comfortable with each other."

They spent a quarter of an hour or so discussing how Charlie had recovered from his accident. Jen reassured Christopher that he was doing all the right things for his young son, especially since the lad no longer had his mother.

"It hasn't been easy, for sure," Christopher said, "but I think I'm moving on now. It's taken me this long to feel ready to move forward after Mia died." He paused. "If I can speak to you in confidence?"

"Absolutely," responded Jen.

"Well, Sally and I have had some fun outings and pleasant times together, and she gets on well with Charlie, of course. Much more, though, she's made me realise that I can be close to someone else again. The time that Mia and I had together was very special. I know I'm a one girl type of bloke, and I thought at one time that what we had was going to be the only relationship I'd ever have. I'll never be able to replace Mia, but I know now that there will be someone else for me." He paused. "I don't think it will be Sally." He shrugged sadly. "But I'm very grateful to her for helping me to see a positive future both for me and for Charlie."

*Poor Sally*, thought Jen. She was not too surprised, though. Jen had thought all along that Christopher was not as keen as she was.

"Anyway, I've yammered on enough. How are you doing these days? You don't look quite so drained. Well, don't say if you don't want to. I don't mean to be nosey, just concerned," he said hastily.

Jen smiled warmly at his interest.

"Mike has come home and swears it won't happen again. We're learning to work it out," she said.

There was a pause which did not seem the slightest bit awkward.

"I have to learn to trust again," she ventured. "It's not easy, and we'll both have to work hard at it. Maybe I was partly to blame too." Jen shrugged disparagingly.

"I have to say, I don't understand it," said Christopher. "I really do wish you well, though. That sounds a bit trite." He frowned. "I mean so much more than that, though."

"Thank you, I understand," said Jen. After a further pause, she said, "I really better be going."

"Yes, of course. I feel we could chatter for ages, but you must be so busy."

"I've enjoyed meeting again, other than at the school door," Jen said with an enthusiasm that surprised her.

*There's a certain comfort in spring,* Jen thought as she headed for her car to return to school. Daffodil leaves were poking through the soil of the neighbouring gardens and there were buds forming in the beech hedge, although the brown leaves were still clinging to the branches, waiting for the new growth to push them off. Celandines were flowering below in the damp coolness and a blue tit, with its bouncing flight, skittered away from its shelter among the dense hedge. Jen smiled to herself, feeling relaxed and happier than she had felt in some time.

*Maybe I'll feel joy again*, she thought. *That's the magic ingredient that's been lacking.*

The following weekend, Jen and Mike were due to visit her mum and dad — Cath and Geoff — for Sunday lunch. They did this on a fairly regular basis, but for no reason in particular they hadn't been for several weeks. Jen was certain she would receive the third degree. She was sure her mum had sensed her lack of complete ease with Mike, despite her best acting the last time they had all been together. They arrived in good time for a pre-lunch drink.

Jen's dad was in his garage, as was often the case. He always had a project on the go for one of the groups he belonged to, or for something around the house or garden. Being retired had not slowed him at all. Mike went out to join him and talk. They got on well. This was another reason Jen had not shared her marital troubles. She didn't want her parents to think less of Mike. She followed her mum into the kitchen, where there was a lovely warmth and the aroma of good food on the go.

"Mmm, smells like pork," she said.

"That's right," said Cath. "With the usual roast potatoes and apple sauce. This time I've done some red cabbage with cranberries and apple mixed in, as well as carrots and beans. It was on one of those cookery things on television and looked good."

"It sounds great. I'm famished," said Jen.

"You always are." Cath laughed. "Pass me the wine bottle, darling. I'll put a splash in the gravy."

They topped up their glasses.

"So what have you two been up to lately?" asked Cath. "Is everything okay?"

*Here we go*, thought Jen. "Everything's fine and much as normal," she replied, feeling this was not too far from the truth, now.

"Only I thought you seemed a little strained last time we were together," Cath continued.

"Mike and I had a bit of up and down in the autumn, but everything's fine now. Probably all this winter weather getting on top of us," she finished somewhat lamely.

"If you ever need to talk or want anything, you know we're always here for you, darling. There's nothing you could say that would shock us. I've seen and heard it all in my time."

"I know, Mum," Jen answered. She turned away on the pretence of replacing the wine bottle as her eyes welled up. "It's fine, really. Love you lots," she added with affection.

Jen knew that ultimately her parents would always support her in any way necessary. It was her feeling of failure that prevented her from sharing the troubles she had experienced.

Turning back, Jen changed the subject. "What's Dad up to now?"

"Oh, you know him. This time he volunteered to make a penny roll table for the village spring fayre. He's enjoyed himself talking endlessly about measurements and angles and which wood to use, and now he's closeted away for hours at a time making it." She laughed.

It wasn't long before they heard Mike and Geoff returning to the house.

"I suspect the beer glasses are empty," Jen said.

Sure enough, as he opened the door Geoff waved his empty glass and asked, "Any more where that came from?"

"Always more," said Cath. "But lunch is just about ready. Do you want to open the new bottle of wine instead?"

"Will do."

They spent a congenial time together, and when it was time to leave Cath managed to get Jen alone again and whispered, "Remember we'll always be here for you."

"Thanks, Mum. Thanks for a lovely lunch," Jen added more loudly as her dad and Mike joined them in the hall. The men shook hands and Geoff gave Jen a big hug.

"Take care, love. Love you. Come whenever you want."

This was uncharacteristically outspoken for him, and Jen knew that her parents must have been discussing her.

As she and Mike went down the path she took her husband's hand, determinedly demonstrating to her watching parents that all was fine.

# CHAPTER 22

There was a surprise awaiting the staff at Holly Road School at the beginning of the following week. Since her mother's health scare before Christmas, Sally had been away from school on several occasions to care for her parent. While everyone was very supportive, there was no doubt that it caused extra work for several people.

Generally Graham, the headteacher, had covered the absence, because money was tight and this saved on the supply teacher budget. However, Jen had usually needed to provide him with the work to be covered, and she talked him through it. This caused the least disruption for the children.

Sally was absent again that day, Jen discovered when she went to her classroom and found Graham there, puzzling over the work documents. During the staff meeting that lunchtime Graham was in his office doing some catch-up work so, as his deputy, Sheila made the surprise announcement. Sally had decided she could no longer cope with the demands of her sick mother and the responsibilities of the classroom. Senior staff and Governors had discussed with her the possibility of taking a part-time contract, but she was adamant that she would prefer to leave. She and her mum were going to move to be closer to her sister, who would then be able to help out more.

There were general groans, sighs and noises of sadness at this decision. Sally was a popular member of staff and well-liked by the children and their parents. It had been decided that as soon as a supply teacher could be found, who would be able to cover until a permanent replacement was appointed, she would be gone.

Jen was sad at the news on several levels. Sally had been very welcoming when Jen had arrived. They had hit it off straight away. It was she who had been a friend when Mary and Lesley had been nasty to her, and they had been good teaching partners, bouncing ideas off each other and working as a strong team professionally.

On a more personal level, Jen reflected upon Sally's blossoming association with Christopher. Following his disclosure to her last week, she understood now that this was a relationship that was going nowhere major, but she wondered if Sally had picked up on this too.

The next day, Sally returned to work. Before school started, there was an opportunity to have a quick chat.

"Sally, I'm really sad that you've decided to go," said Jen with feeling.

"I don't exactly want to," she replied, "but things are impossible at the moment. I feel I'm only doing half a job both at home and at school."

"Where will you go?"

"My sister lives with her family just outside Bradford in Yorkshire, so we're going to rent somewhere up there while we sort out selling the house here." Then Sally went on to answer the unspoken question on Jen's mind. "I had hoped I might be the one for Christopher, but I don't think that's going to happen either. We get on well enough, but he's someone who needs a lifetime soulmate, I'm sure of that now. I think he's ready to move on, just not with me." She sighed and shrugged. Then on a brighter note, she said, "Bradford will be a new start. It's a university city with lots going on. It's probably the change I need."

"Well, I'm really going to miss you," Jen said sincerely.

"Thanks, Jen. It's been good working with you too. I've learned loads of stuff from you, and I'm sure in time I'll get another job and build on what I've picked up here."

With that, Sally left for her own classroom and Jen turned to get on with her morning.

The term progressed, a supply teacher was found, and Jen was busy helping to induct her into the school and her class. She missed Sally and her camaraderie, but the new teacher, Kim Sutton, was only slightly older than Jen and they seemed to get on well. Kim had a young family and was looking to get back into full-time teaching, so she was prepared to work hard and took on board suggestions that Jen made.

Easter came and went, and Jen found she had been at Holly Road School for nearly a year. So much had happened both at school and at home, and it seemed hardly credible that summer was nearly upon them again.

Things with Mike had chugged along. Jen was still hurting, but she was determined to try and regain the trust that she had lost so bitterly. Mike was continuing as if nothing had occurred. Whilst she felt damaged and deeply hurt, he'd moved on because it was over, and that was that.

On Saturdays he usually went off to the gym while she stayed at home, often catching up on school work so that she wasn't doing so much when he was around. Sometimes he was out one evening a week, but while she was uneasy she quelled any suspicious thoughts. To be fair, he gave her no cause to doubt him.

One Friday morning, Jen had to be at school in good time because she had a meeting with a parent before the children arrived and, unusually, she was ready to leave before Mike. Normally he was gone first, and so there was no need to shuffle cars about. On this morning he was still only half dressed, so she took his keys from the hook as well as hers and prepared to move his car out of the way so that she could get hers out. She unlocked the driver's door and getting in, she started the engine. It had been a cold night, and her breath immediately steamed up the window. She looked in the door pocket for a cloth to wipe the window but couldn't find it. Then she remembered she had probably used it last when they had gone together to the supermarket the previous weekend.

She leant over to rummage in the passenger door pocket — and that's when she smelled it. She sat upright quickly, shaking slightly. Surely she was wrong. She leaned over again and sniffed. She wasn't mistaken. It certainly wasn't her perfume. She pulled the passenger seatbelt towards her and smelled the distinctive aroma of Diana's perfume. She was so familiar with it she was quite certain that's what it was.

Her mind was racing. There could be all sorts of explanations. Maybe Mike had given one of the office girls a lift to the bus stop or the shopping centre. Lots of people probably used this scent. She took several deep breaths to calm her shaking, which was violent now. He had told her it was over. He hadn't been out that much lately. When had they last made love? It was at the weekend. He was out last night, but not that late. He had rushed out as soon as they had eaten, though. Had he rushed or just gone out? She had to get to work. She had to calm down. There must be a rational explanation. She mustn't judge so quickly.

She moved the cars, ran into the house to drop his keys on the worktop and shouted up the stairs to say she was going. She couldn't face this now. She must calm down and take her time to decide properly what line to take. Perhaps she should ignore it. No, but she had to think what to do. She mustn't blindly accuse. There might be an innocent reason. It would not be at all helpful if that was the case and she had jumped in with both feet. As she drove to work, she gradually talked herself into believing there was nothing to worry about. She would think further and maybe sleep on it before asking Mike where the perfume had come from.

Following her appointment and after welcoming the children into the classroom, that morning Jen had some non-contact time for which she was very grateful. She tried to concentrate on the planning and preparation that she knew she had to get done. For a while, her work completely stopped her mind from racing down a blind alley. During the second part of the morning, Kim joined her and they continued to prepare for the following week while the higher level teaching assistants took their classes. It was good to be bouncing ideas off each other, and several times they laughed together. Jen liked Kim, and she was turning into a real asset to the school and to Jen in particular, especially on this particular morning.

By the end of the school afternoon, Jen was much more calm and ready to leave the talk with Mike until the weekend. She would choose her moment and not be accusatory in any way. With these thoughts, she drove home, stopping to get a takeaway she could re-heat and a bottle of wine from the supermarket.

That evening, they both chilled out on the sofa. Jen had to admit that Mike seemed perfectly normal in the way that he spoke to her, and the more she thought about it the more distant her fears seemed to be.

# CHAPTER 23

The next morning, being Saturday, Mike went to the gym as usual. Jen squashed all unwelcome thoughts and set about getting on with some school work. She hadn't been going for long when the doorbell rang. As she walked up the hallway, she could see the vague outline of someone tall through the glass, so she guessed who it was and wondered uneasily why he had come.

"Hello, Greg," Jen said, smiling as best she could and standing back to hold open the door. "Come on in."

"I hope I'm not interrupting too much. I assumed that Mike would be at the gym," he started.

"You assumed correctly. Do you want a coffee?" Jen asked, putting off the moment of asking what he wanted.

"Yes, thanks. You look great, Jen. How are you?" Greg responded, similarly hesitant to start the conversation.

"I'm okay," she said vaguely. "I was just doing some school work."

"Sorry," he said. "I just needed to ask you something."

"Well, fire away," Jen said, trying to sound enthusiastic.

"It's awkward. Okay, here goes. Is everything alright again with you and Mike?"

Jen paused and then put down the coffee jar. She turned and put her hand on Greg's arm. "Why do you ask?" she questioned gently.

"It's just that I thought Diana and I were getting back on track, but now she seems distant again and I don't know what to do. Should I back off and give her more time; should I move out, even?"

"Greg, I really don't know what to say. Mike and I have been getting on better, I think."

Jen really didn't know whether to express her concerns of the day before. She finally decided not to. After all, she didn't have anything to say, did she? She had no evidence of wrongdoing on Mike's part at all.

"I'm really sorry to bother you," said Greg, frowning and awkward.

"Oh, come here," Jen said and stepped towards him, her arms wide to console him. He had been a very good friend to her and it was upsetting to see him so distressed

"I said once before I should have met you first, Jen," he said. "You're so steadfast and genuine."

Jen was unsure quite how to respond, so she said nothing and after a moment or two more she released him and turned to finish making the coffee.

"Maybe you need to give it more time, Greg. Or maybe you need to talk to Diana and ask her what she's feeling. I'm certainly no expert, but all the professionals you read about say that communication is the thing that many relationships lack. I'm afraid I'm really not the person to ask. I don't seem to be very good at it, do I?" She shrugged and sighed.

"You're right, though, of course. I should be asking Diana rather than you," Greg admitted. "Thanks," he added as he took his cup of coffee.

He didn't stay long after he had finished his drink. He kissed her forehead and squeezed her arm at the door.

"Do keep in touch, Jen. I should hate all this to part us as well."

"I will, and it won't," Jen said, and she meant it.

After she had closed the front door, Jen returned to her seat at the table and sat staring at her work. She realised she was chewing the end of her pencil and mentally shook herself. It didn't seem long after when she heard Mike's key in the lock, so she started to pack away her things without really completing very much. She needed to decide what, if anything, to do and how to tackle the big question in her mind. Had Mike seen Diana again?

Her opening came more quickly than she expected, but she was couldn't decide whether to take it or not.

"Has someone been?" Mike straightened up from depositing his gym clothes in the washing machine. He was looking in the sink, where the two empty coffee cups were lying.

"Greg called round," Jen said.

"Oh." He paused. "And what did *he* want?"

Was Jen imagining it, or did Mike seem ill at ease about this? Then again, this could be a natural reaction because of past events and the uneasy relationship Mike and Greg now presumably had. These thoughts flitted fleetingly through Jen's mind. "He called round to see how I was," she answered.

"Why would he do that?"

"I suppose because we've been friends and we haven't seen him for ages," she said.

"Mmm," Mike grunted and left the room to go upstairs.

Now that her opportunity had passed, Jen perversely wished she had taken it. Now she would need to let it go or engineer another opportunity. She mentally kicked herself for being so uncharacteristically feeble.

As she leant against the sink, something else passed through her mind. Mike had put his gear in the machine for washing, but he hadn't switched it on. Should she take it out and look at it to see if, indeed, he had used it? Oh, for goodness' sake! She really should not spy on her own husband. On the other hand, what had caused her to act like this, if not his behaviour towards her? Without further debate with herself, she leant down and pulled out his shirt. It was bone dry, and despite being rumpled it still had the crease marks in it from when she had ironed it. Shaking, she forced herself to pull out a sock. Again it was sweet-smelling, dry and unstained. Quickly she shoved the things back in the machine and propped herself up against the sink.

She heard the toilet flush upstairs and Mike's footsteps descending. Hyperaware of his movements, she heard him go into the living room and then she heard him approaching the kitchen. She wanted to shrink down onto the floor and dissolve. Somehow she gripped the sink tightly, took several deep breaths and then turned to look at him as he entered the room.

"Are you alright?" he asked.

"Where did you go this morning?" Jen's hands were shaking, so she placed them behind her as she leaned against the sink and tried to sound casual and friendly.

"To the hotel, where the gym is," Mike answered, smiling — or was he smirking at his own cleverness?

"Okay," Jen said coldly, her anger spilling out. "To use the gym or to do something else?"

"What do you mean?"

"You know what I mean. Be honest with me, at least. You haven't used your gym stuff, and why was Diana's perfume on your passenger seatbelt?"

"So you've been checking up on me have you?" Was he playing for time? Probably.

"Seems like I needed to," Jen responded coldly. Anger exploded again, this time violently, and she felt as if her whole being was being seized and dashed against the floor. She kicked the cupboard uncontrollably and banged the worktop with her hand. "You told me it was over. She was my friend, you bastard. You couldn't even make a move more distant. It's despicable," she shouted.

"Jen, please, let me explain."

"Explain? How can you explain this?" Jen was sobbing now.

"She rang me last week. She needed a lift to the hospital. Her sister is really ill and Greg was away on business. She was really upset; too upset to drive safely, so I said I'd take her. She said there was no-one else she could ask. One thing just led to another. I'm really sorry, Jen."

"Go, get out now, as soon as you can pack. I don't want to discuss this."

"Jen, please, it was a one-off. It is over, really," he pleaded.

Jen turned her back. "I want you to leave," she said.

He left the room and she heard him go upstairs. There was quite a lot of banging around, and a while later, she heard him descend. She had stayed where she was in the kitchen, gripping the sink. She didn't want to speak to him again at this point in time, and she prayed he wouldn't seek her out again.

"Jen..." He was at the kitchen door, but she didn't answer and didn't turn. She couldn't bring herself to respond. She felt rather than heard him turn away, and then she heard the front door open and bang shut.

Later, she wasn't sure how much later, she put on her short jacket and taking her keys she headed up the road. She needed a friendly face and a warm welcome. Pat answered her front door and seeing Jen's face, without a word she held it wide. Immediately tears welled in Jen's eyes again. She felt as if she had been consistently downhearted for several months. Nothing seemed to be going right.

Pat went into the kitchen and Jen followed. Sitting at the table, she put her head in her hands and cried. Pat said nothing but let the flow continue. Joe came in.

"Hello, Jen. What's the matter?"

"Jen's upset but she's come here, and we'll make her feel better, won't we?" Pat answered him.

"Sorry, Jen," said the young lad, not really knowing quite what to do.

Jen smiled wetly at him.

"Don't worry, I'll be fine when I've spoken with your mum and had a cup of tea," she reassured Joe, seeing his worried expression. It was not normal to see grown-ups like this.

"Can you go and fetch the box of tissues from the bathroom?" Pat said to her son, understanding that he needed a job to do and giving Jen a quick moment of respite.

"I'm really sorry," said Jen, slowly gathering herself.

"He'll be fine," answered Pat. She brought two mugs of tea to the table. "If in doubt or when upset, always have a cup of tea. Want to talk about it?"

"Yes, if you can stand another round of depression."

"We seem to spend quite a bit of time propping up each other," said Pat.

"He's gone again," Jen said simply. "He told me it was over, but clearly it wasn't or she wasn't out of his system. He saw her again. I guessed something and then the evidence was there." Jen explained the sequence of recent events. "It is reasonable, isn't it, to want a partner who is faithful and trustworthy?"

"Some men are definitely monogamous," said Pat. "But it seems that more are not. It depends what you want and can accept."

"What about you?" Jen sipped her tea.

"I have the boys to think about as well as myself, although that's all tied up together. You know Doug and I have been apart for some time now, but the boys miss him and actually, so do I. I think he loves us in his way, but he's basically a selfish person and his desires come first. I have to decide whether I can put up with that."

"Mmm, I see, I think," said Jen, although she didn't fully comprehend Pat's point of view.

Pat continued, "He's good company. We do make quite a good team, especially where the boys are concerned. I miss him. Maybe for the times he's not totally here, if you get my drift, I have to rely on my own resources more. Anyway, as he gets older I think he'll find it's hard work being deceitful and maybe not worth the effort. After all, he does have a basically lazy streak." Half a smile appeared on her face as she appeared to reflect.

Jen found it hard to take this on board, but she was content to sit and soak up the atmosphere of Pat's house and to be wrapped in their friendship. She knew beyond all doubt that Pat would never deceive her. There were some people who could be genuine friends.

Having got herself under control and having shared her problems, Jen began to feel more able to cope with the situation. Eventually she said her thanks and goodbyes to Pat. She also popped her head around the living room door to see the two boys.

"I'm off now, and as you see your mum has worked her magic and I'm fine." She smiled at them. "See you soon." She blew them a kiss.

She walked back along the road to her own house. When she arrived at her door, she nearly stepped on the small bundle of fluff curled up in the corner of the front step.

"Hello," she said as she bent down to stroke the cat. In fact, it was almost still a kitten. It was a beautiful creamy white with smaller ginger patches on its ears, back and tail. "What are you doing here? You don't live with me, I'm afraid."

Jen opened her front door. The young cat made to come in but Jen knew, much as she would like to make a fuss of it, if she did it would stay forever, and it must have a home somewhere nearby. It wouldn't be fair on the real owners to tempt it away. Someone would be very upset. She hardened her heart and closed the door on it. She spent a lonely evening in front of the television, feeling like having a glass of wine but resisting the temptation.

On Sunday, Jen mooched around the house, making herself do the jobs that had to be done. She found it hard to concentrate and fluctuated between dismal depression and anger.

The little cat was not there first thing in the morning but reappeared later on in the day. Again, she determined not to encourage it, but she felt that she would just love to give it some food and a gentle cuddle. It was so endearing.

On Tuesday morning, it was there again and Jen really thought it was looking slightly more grey and less well cared for. It mewed pitifully when she left for school, and she couldn't resist bending to stroke it tenderly.

"Go home, little one. I have to go to work," she whispered to it.

After school, Jen had arranged to go and see Mrs Jarvis, the mother of a girl in her class. Six years old, Tina Jarvis lived with her mum in a small terraced house on the housing estate at the back of the school. Tina was a lovely little girl but was often teased for being very overweight. One day, she had been wearing a pink hand-knitted cardigan.

"Tina you look like a lovely, delicious pink ice-cream. I could just eat you up," Jen had said to her.

The class had tittered, but their attitude to the child had changed with that one remark. Mrs Jarvis tried hard to support Tina but didn't find it easy on her own and tended to overcompensate and do far too much for her. This lady was renowned all through school for her malapropisms. These word muddles had caused quite a bit of mirth on occasions, so although Jen was really tired she didn't mind visiting and wanted to support this caring mum. Mrs Jarvis did everything for Tina, to the extent that the child had no idea how to organise herself, even in the simplest of activities.

Sometimes Jen took a teaching assistant with her on home visits, for her own safety or to ensure the correct outcome was recorded, but this time it wasn't necessary. When she knocked, Mrs Jarvis opened the door and beamed her bountiful smile.

"'Ello, me duck, come on in," she said in her East Midlands accent. "Cuppa tea?"

"No, I'm fine," Jen said.

"You're right on time, duck. I like good *punctuation*. Shows seriousness. Righto, then, let's crack on and get down to *brass roots*," said Mrs Jarvis.

Jen smiled. "I think we need to help Tina be a little more consistent in her timing and to be a bit more organised in her work. That way, she'll make better progress," she began.

"Aw, I know how *erotic* she can be, never doing the same thing twice in the same way. Is it a *pigment* of my imagination, or is she getting a bit better, though?" Mrs Jarvis asked.

They managed to agree some simple short-term targets revolving around Tina doing things for herself rather than her mum doing absolutely everything for her.

"I only want to protect 'er. I don't want 'er to end up like me," said Mrs Jarvis in her flamboyant manner. "I mean, Mum always said to me, 'Don't you get yourself into trouble, young lady. Saying no is the best form of *contraption*.' Before I knew it, I was in the family way." There followed a loud guffaw. "The thought of her ending up with a kiddie at that age, well, it puts the willies up me."

At this last remark and given the context, Jen had great difficulty in keeping a straight face but managed to make a gentle, comforting comment.

Feeling that, at least, she had made positive contact and started to outline the problem and possible solutions, Jen drove back to school.

"I thought you'd gone for today," said Jim, the caretaker, as she entered the front door and skipped over the hoover.

"I've been to visit a parent, and I just want to do a bit in the classroom for tomorrow," Jen replied. "I shan't be too late."

"That's okay. I've got the Beaver Scouts in tonight, remember, so the building'll be open for ages yet."

An hour or so later, Jen had gathered her things, collected some work to keep her busy through the evening and got in her car to drive home. On arriving, she staggered to the door, her arms full. Putting down her bags, she was surprised to see that the little cat was, again, outside her door. This time, when she turned the key and opened the door, it dived in ahead of her as she stooped to retrieve her bags.

"Hey, you rascal," she called, dumping her stuff down in the hall. She hurried to find the cat, which had jumped onto the sofa and looked up at her with big eyes.

"Right, I can see I'm going to have to make enquiries about you."

Jen really wanted to give it some food. It was definitely looking more unkempt this evening. She stroked its soft back and gently massaged the back of its neck behind its pretty ears. Immediately it began to purr and Jen warmed to it. She knew if she fed it, that would be that. It would be happy to make its home with her and quite content to abandon any family it might already have.

"I'm going to see if I can find out where you belong, though," she said to the little cat as she carried it through to the kitchen and found a small dish in which to put a drop of milk. "I know older cats are not supposed to have milk but I haven't anything else this minute, and you do look very hungry."

After it had licked every drop, the young cat mooched into the living room and curled up on the floor with its back against the sofa.

"Well, you look very comfy," Jen whispered to it. "But I'm just going to nip around to the shop and put a note in their window. I'd love to keep you, but if you do belong somewhere else, you really better go back home. Your owners might be upset if you just disappear."

Jen quickly whipped up a poster on her laptop, printed off several copies and walked to the little parade of shops. Only the small supermarket was still open, but she asked if they would put the poster in their window and left a copy for the post office, which shared the same premises. While returning home, she wondered where else she could advertise this find.

The young cat spent the evening with her, giving her comfort and making her feel needed.

"It sounds dopey, I know, but..." she said to the cat, "I really like having you here."

She put it outside last thing at night, and then she went to bed and cried a waterfall into the pillows. Why had this happened to her? All she wanted was someone to love her exclusively, as she had loved in return.

# CHAPTER 24

Following her enquiries at the local shops and after asking various neighbours about the little cat's ownership, Jen had turned up no information at all. She had eventually decided that it must be a case of it having been dumped. Jen had verified that it was a female, so she had taken her to the local vet for a 'once over' and to organise spaying. She had also bought all the accoutrements she might need. The cat's colour led to her name, Fudge. They had quickly become good companions, and now Jen couldn't imagine the house without her little friend. She was there when Jen came home from work, purring and winding herself around her legs. She kept her company during some long, otherwise lonely evenings.

Spring eventually turned to summer. Mike rang Jen occasionally, but she had no wish to have a long and involved conversation. She was putting off the moment, she knew, and procrastinating so that painful decisions did not need to be made. He had gone back to stay with Alex, but he wouldn't be able to stay there forever.

Jen saw Greg once or twice. One Saturday morning, he called round and they went for a coffee at the local pub. The next time he came was early one evening.

"Do you fancy going for a stroll? I was at a loose end, and it's such lovely weather," he said.

They walked along the streets and talked, inevitably, about their combined situation.

"Diana's moved out of the flat and gone to live on the other side of town," he said.

*That should make things easier for Mike,* Jen thought bitterly. "I don't know if they're still seeing each other," Jen said. "I don't think I want to know."

"Let's change the subject," Greg said.

They ended up at the tiny local park, where there were swings and a small slide. Sitting on a bench, Greg laid his arm along the back behind Jen, but he didn't touch her, and she enjoyed the evening.

Another time, they drove out of town on one grey, wet evening and went for a drink at a country pub. Jen even found herself laughing at a tale Greg told of his work colleague, who had been on a flight to Edinburgh and got into all kinds of tangles with elderly co-passengers and their carry-on baggage. He finished the long-winded story and Jen was giggling, unsure whether it was the story, the effects of two glasses of wine, or the release of months of tension. Greg then capitalised with the corniest of jokes.

"As migration approached, two elderly vultures doubted they could make the trip south, so they decided to go by aeroplane. When they checked their baggage, the attendant noticed that they were carrying two dead squirrels. 'Do you wish to check the squirrels through as luggage?' she asked. 'No, thanks,' replied the vultures. 'They're carrion!'" he finished.

"Greg, that's appalling," Jen laughed.

"I know, but I prefer that to the rude type. Probably dull, but there it is, that's me," he said sardonically.

"Not dull," Jen said and leaned across to give his arm a squeeze, thinking that he was such a nice man.

They drove home in companionable silence. When they got back to Jen's house, she was tempted to ask him in for coffee, but that always had other meanings on television and in films, and she wasn't sure how to cope with situations like that. Her position was saved by Greg being practical and helpful yet again.

"If I come in for coffee," he said, smiling, "don't worry, that's all I would expect. I know how awkward this situation could become."

"Thanks, Greg. Please come in … for coffee," Jen laughed back at him.

They continued a pleasant evening, and when it was time for him to leave, Greg turned to Jen at the front door and planted a light kiss on her lips. Jen closed the door thoughtfully.

Having taken the empty cups into the kitchen and left them in the sink, she floated off to bed and lay for a long time, going over the evening in her mind and considering all kinds of possibilities. She liked Greg a lot, but did she feel more than that, or was she just welcoming the reassurance that his attentions gave her? She desperately needed to feel wanted and valued. Fudge snuggled by her feet, quietly purring.

As she lay, Jen's mind drifted to her parents. She had finally visited them to divulge the awful news of her and Mike's break-up. Typically her parents had rallied around and been totally supportive when she'd broken down in tears and told of her feelings of failure and inadequacy. Jen was grateful her mum had resisted calling Mike names, when she explained her understanding that it wouldn't help her daughter. No-one knew what the future held for the pair. They were still married. Pat had taken Doug back into their home again, after all.

Tears came, yet again, and Jen dashed them away and sat up to stroke Fudge until they had gone.

The end of term came, and the summer holidays started. Jen had been at the school for a whole year. She knew she had settled well there. She had made good in-roads into both raising standards in her classroom and ensuring progress with her home/school liaison responsibility. She was well respected and liked by the headteacher, other staff and parents and pupils.

In May, she had been invited to be involved in the interview process for Sally's replacement. This had been a new but very good experience for her. There had been three candidates, one of whom was Kim Sutton, and it had been she who had got the position. She had interviewed honestly and assuredly, and they were confident about offering her the job. Jen had found the experience stimulating but difficult. However, she was very pleased with the outcome, even though she was not involved in the final decision, having worked so closely with Kim.

Jen had been fully immersed in all the end-of-term processes too. There were end-of-year parent/teacher consultations at which she received many compliments, sports days, the leavers' assembly and evening discos for the children. Then there were the oldest pupils for whom they all signed shirts and said goodbye as they moved on to the secondary school. She had been sorry to say goodbye to her own class as well. They had made good progress and she had exceeded her targets with them, but more than that, they'd had fun and she felt close to them.

She was particularly sad to say farewell to Charlie, for whom she had a special fondness which had developed quickly following his accident. He had made a superb recovery and his dad was very pleased indeed with his progress; a fact that he had voiced in no uncertain terms at parents' evening and since. Still, while she wouldn't be responsible for them, she would see them again in September when, no doubt, they would all seem suddenly older and ready for Year 2. It had been a busy time, but it had kept Jen's mind off her home problems.

When Mike had first left, Jen had been in tears on a daily basis. Through late spring and early summer, she had frequently taken herself for a walk in the early evening; across the fields behind the house, over the bridge crossing the little brook and back along the streets. More often than not, she'd found herself having a good cry, which had been regularly repeated when she was alone in bed. This was no longer a daily occurrence, however. Now the holidays were here, and at the start she had made up her mind to keep as busy as possible to hold the miseries at bay.

Jen decided to go shopping during the first week. She was going to buy new bedding and clear out the bedroom. No more of this crying into pillows. She had awoken really early and so got up in good time too. It was a beautiful morning. After she had showered, she put on a light, strappy summer dress with her flat sandals. She brushed her hair and only applied a little eye make-up and lip gloss. The sun on the playground during the last part of the term had given her a lovely tan and she was beginning to look healthier. She decided to drive into the bigger town to look at the linen in the department store.

The walls of her room at home were powder-blue and white, so she wanted something to complement that. She wandered around the displays, debating whether to go for something strong and contrasting, and if so, what colours should she choose? On her second round, she spied exactly what she was looking for. The set was plain white with small, blue embroidered flowers dotted here and there. It was crisp and clean-looking. She selected the size she needed and took it to the counter to pay.

Looking at her watch, she decided to head to the cafeteria for a cup of tea and maybe even a scone. She felt like having a treat. Holding two bags, she was concentrating hard on balancing her tray with its little teapot, cup and plate when there was a voice over her shoulder.

"You look like you need another pair of hands. Can I help?"

As Jen turned, her hair whipped across her eyes and a strand caught in her mouth. He gently took it and tucked it behind her ear. It was so naturally done that it made her tummy flip. She smiled into his eyes, those twinkling, green eyes, and managed to mumble a thank you as he took her tray.

"Perhaps you would join us?" Christopher asked as he headed to a table where Charlie sat waiting for his dad to return with a serviette to mop his son's mouth.

Jen followed, mesmerised by Christopher's retreating back, admiring his broad shoulders and his shirt, slightly untucked from the jeans that hung from his narrow hips. "Thank you, yes," she said vaguely.

"Hello, Charlie," Jen greeted the little boy.

He beamed at her. "Are you going to sit there?" he asked, indicating the seat opposite him.

"Yes, thank you."

"We're having an away-day, my dad said," Charlie chirped. "After here we're going to the park and we're going on the train and we're going to have chips for lunch."

Christopher smiled indulgently at his son. "How are you?" He turned his green eyes to Jen.

"I'm getting there," she answered. "I'm on my own again now. I have been since the beginning of April."

"Oh, my goodness," Christopher said sincerely. "I did wonder how it was going."

"Well, it's not, is the short answer," Jen shrugged. "It all kicked off again, and so there we are." She glanced at Charlie.

"Now isn't the time for details," Christopher acknowledged. "But are you coping?"

"I wasn't for a while, but I'm starting to now," Jen said. "I've just been buying a new duvet cover and pillow cases, and then I thought I'd have a treat in here. Tomorrow I'm going to have a good, if late, spring clean upstairs."

"Have you any plans for the rest of today?" Christopher asked. "We'd love it if you joined us. It's not high-octane, but as Charlie says we're treating ourselves today, and doing some really mischievous things, like chips for lunch." He smiled and cocked his head at his son.

Jen hesitated for only a moment. "What the heck," she said. "Why not? It's only me now, so I might as well please myself. I'd love to."

They finished their drinks and snacks and arranged to meet in the car park for the steam train station. They would catch the train to the country park, spend the day there, having their chips for lunch, and catch the train back again. It all sounded fun. Jen was quite excited at the prospect.

The day was glorious, uncomplicated and relaxed. Charlie chattered non-stop and Jen and Christopher were much the same. The steam train stopped on its journey to let them off at the park. They went to the swings and climbing frames. Then they all paddled in the lake and then ran around on the grass playing chase to dry their sandy feet. After their lunch, Jen and Christopher sat quietly and had a cup of tea outside so that they could watch Charlie while he fed the remains of his chips to the geese and ducks down by the water's edge. The sun sparkled on the water's ripples and warmed Jen's face as she sat, relaxing her.

She divulged her recent history to Christopher, and they chatted comfortably about living alone. Jen felt it was easier for her now that, officially, Charlie was not in her direct care at school, although there was no law against having a friendship with one of the parents. The afternoon passed companionably and very quickly. So soon, it seemed, it was time to head back to the little station to catch the steam train back to where they had left their cars.

As it pulled in and stopped with a loud, prolonged hiss, Jen breathed in the scent of the steam and coal. It was many years since she had taken this ride. The last time had probably been when she was a child. It brought back happy memories. Charlie was hopping from one foot to the other now, clearly anticipating the ride back with similar feelings.

Having returned they stood, each next to their own car, ready to head home.

"This has been a lovely day," said Jen.

"It wasn't exactly 'treating a lady', but I'm afraid it's what Charlie and I do," Christopher responded with a wry shrug.

"I've loved every minute of it. I truly have," said Jen and she meant it.

There was a pause. Jen was about to turn to unlock her car and say her final farewells when Christopher spoke again.

"I don't suppose you would have dinner with me one night, would you? It would have to be at my house because of Charlie, but I'd love to cook for you. That's if you would like to, of course. I quite understand if you don't feel ready… I mean, if you need to consider your options for longer, under the circumstances…" He trailed off, realising he was babbling.

Jen smiled. "I'd love to," she said quickly, surprising herself.

Christopher exhaled deeply, and they both realised he had been tensed up, ready to ask her but afraid of rejection. "Well, it's Monday today — what about Wednesday? That would give me time to plan and shop."

"Wednesday it is. What time shall I come? I don't mind coming early and helping to peel or chop things."

"Absolutely not, on this occasion. I shall try to impress you with my culinary skills." Christopher laughed. "Come about seven-thirty. Charlie will be ready for bed and he can say goodnight before we eat."

"I'll see you on Wednesday, then. Thank you." She turned to Charlie and bent down to his level. "Thank you, Charlie, for a wonderful day and the best plate of chips I've had in ages."

"It was great. Thank you," he answered.

As she drove home, Jen reflected on all that had happened. It had been a truly great outing. As she pulled up outside her house, she found she was grinning to herself.

That evening, Jen made up her bed with the new linen and as she lay within its coolness, she was still going over the day and all that it had held.

# CHAPTER 25

Wednesday evening came around quickly. The day had been sunny and warm with large white clouds in the blue sky. Jen did her cleaning and clearing the day before and finished off during the morning. During her activities, she had felt sad at the loss of what she'd had and then angry at the betrayal she'd endured.

After, she'd had a long, very hot shower and washed all those feelings away. She felt good, more positive and looking forward to the evening with Christopher Mayhew.

On her arrival, she heard Charlie running to the front door to open it.

"Hello," he cried. "Come in. Daddy's in the kitchen and he said I could open the door."

As she entered, Christopher came into the hall, wiping his hands with a tea towel. Jen could smell something delicious and her mouth started to water. Christopher sounded quite calm as he greeted her with a big smile and said to Charlie, "Will you take Jen's jacket and lay it on my bed?"

His slightly dishevelled appearance belied his demeanour.

"Daddy said if I asked you politely, you might read me a story before I go to bed," Charlie said.

"Maybe we should let Jen get inside the door first and take a breath." Christopher laughed amiably. "Sorry. If you'd rather not…"

"Of course I will. It's all part of bedtime, having a story," Jen responded.

"I shan't be long in the kitchen if you want to go and choose a book," said Christopher. "Nothing too long tonight,

Charlie," he added, giving his son a look, then to Jen: "Don't let him take advantage."

"Don't worry, I won't. I've got his measure." She smiled.

"Of course you have," Christopher acknowledged. "You know him well."

Straight away the atmosphere was relaxed and easy. Jen sat on the sofa and read Charlie's book with him as he leant into her. He'd chosen *Dazzling Diggers*, which was a rhyming book. Before the end, Christopher joined them and sat on the other side of the little boy, looking across at the last few pages as Jen read.

"There you are," she said as she closed the book and tapped Charlie on the knee with it.

"Righto, lad, say night-night." Christopher nodded at his son.

"Can't I just have one more? We quite often have two books," he said, turning his large eyes to Jen.

"That's it for tonight," she said. "Daddy said just the one, so off you go." She grinned, not taken in for one moment by the appealing look he was giving her.

"Okay," he said slowly. "Goodnight." He stretched up to receive a goodnight kiss.

She kissed his forehead and said, "Sleep tight, Charlie, see you again soon."

Christopher returned from tucking up the little boy.

"Thank you," he said. "He thinks the world of you." Before Jen could respond, he continued, "Shall we go through to the other room?"

Jen followed Christopher through to a kitchen-cum-dining room. The area was compact, but all the toys were in a box in the corner and Jen could see that Christopher had tried hard to make the room inviting, with flowers in a vase at one end of the table. Although the sun was still on its descent outside, a candle cast a flickering light in the middle. She was charmed by his efforts.

"Please, do sit down," he said, pouring Jen a glass of wine from a bottle already on the table. "I'm just going to get our first course dished up."

As she sipped the cool wine and he moved about in the kitchen, they chatted easily. Christopher placed a cold crudité of vegetables in the middle of the table between them and small dishes of different dipping sauces that he said he had made himself.

"I hope you don't mind using fingers for this," he said.

"You've been very busy."

"Charlie enjoyed helping, but it would pass all the health and safety regs, so don't worry. I watched him carefully."

Jen normally had a healthy appetite and she certainly did this food justice. "This is so moreish," she said. "I love this sweet and sour sauce, and the pink one. Is that Thousand Island?"

"Mmmhmm,," he answered.

The meal continued. Christopher proved himself to be a very good cook with unflappable calm in the kitchen, and Jen ate heartily and with enjoyment.

"I'm really glad you enjoyed it." Christopher cleared away her empty plate. "I wasn't sure what to cook, so I played it safe with chicken chasseur. Would you like a top-up?" He indicated her glass.

"No, I better not. One glass should be enough. Driving, and all that. It was delicious," Jen said. "As you see by the amount I've eaten."

"Would you like a soft drink, then?" That organised, he continued, "What about some cheeses, or we made a gateaux … or both?"

He laughed and Jen could see a dimple appear at the side of his mouth. Why hadn't she noticed that before?

"Then there's coffee and we made some of our own sweets to go with it."

"My goodness, I am being spoiled," Jen said after a moment's pause.

The evening continued pleasurably. They didn't finish eating until nearly eleven because they were talking so much between courses.

As he cleared the table, prior to serving the coffee, Jen watched as Christopher moved between table and sink. There was something erotic about his broad-shouldered, slim-hipped figure with a tea towel flung carelessly over one shoulder. Earlier, she had made to get up and help, but he had insisted that this time, as it was the first visit, she was to remain seated and waited upon. Next time, he had said, she could help.

*Next time*, she had thought to herself happily.

She admired his strong, capable-looking hands, with their long fingers and just a few fine dark hairs on his forearms that continued up under his rolled-up cuffs. She looked again at his broad shoulders and while he wasn't tall, not as tall as Mike — the thought came unbidden — he was well proportioned and attractive. His eyes had sparkled with the candle flame as the light outside disappeared.

Jen followed Christopher through to the little sitting room as he carried a tray with coffee, cups, cream and sugar. He put it carefully down on a table in front of the sofa and indicated that she might sit down there. She sat at one end, suddenly feeling vulnerable and awkward. He sat on the sofa too, but at the other end with a respectable distance between them. Having poured the coffee, he must have sensed her discomfiture.

"I think, maybe, I understand how you feel. It has taken me several years, until now in fact, to feel at ease with moving on with my life. I was in a complete wilderness after Mia died. I imagine you might be feeling a mixture of guilt and unease."

"Yes, some of that," Jen answered. "I've spent months walking in the evenings and at weekends, and sometimes the weather has been joyous. There have been blue skies, birds singing, warmth and calm, but I felt no joy, none at all. I began to wonder if I was depressed. That's something from which I never thought I'd suffer. I'm still married and I took the vows I made really seriously. Now, though, I think I feel they no longer stand because of what Mike has done and then done *again*, but I feel confused."

"I recognise all of that," Christopher said. "I think it can be one of the stages of a break-up. I know it is one of the stages of mourning. At first I was in denial and then incredibly angry. I had my moments of crying, even," he admitted. "I understand how you feel. You will find peace. I just want to say that I shan't make any demands upon you until you're ready. It's just that I know how *I* feel, and I'd like us to meet again. I value you too much to ask for more than you can give."

"Thank you." Jen looked down at her hands and then met his eyes. "Thank you," she said again.

The moment of Jen's awkwardness left as soon as it had come and while they sipped their coffee, general chat resumed. Jen was able to talk openly of her married life and Christopher mentioned his wife's name with ease. The next hour passed without either of them realising the time, until Jen glanced at the clock on the mantelpiece and was shocked at how late it was.

"I must go," she gasped. "Look at the time."

As she stood by the front door with her jacket on, she thanked Christopher. In a rather lovely old-fashioned way, he asked if he could kiss her goodnight. As her answer, she raised her face to him. He placed his hands on either side of her face and gently kissed her forehead and then lowered his lips to hers. The kiss was firm and dry, and Jen's breath slipped away with the raging beats of her heart.

"Ring me when you are ready, if you want to," he whispered. "Goodnight."

# CHAPTER 26

Greg called round the weekend following Jen's dinner date. It was Saturday morning. She asked herself why he had chosen that particular time and wondered if it was because he knew that Mike would definitely not be calling in. Saturday morning was his gym session.

Maybe, Jen thought, she was reading too much into things. It was just that last time Greg had left, he had grabbed a kiss from her and while it had been fairly passionless, it had been aimed at her lips.

This time they chatted amiably about this and that. Jen was beginning to speculate why he had come when he finally asked her to dinner. She took a gulp of her coffee to give herself time to think and make an appropriate response.

"Dinner?" she asked. Then, taking a deep breath, she ploughed on. "Greg, I don't think that would be a good idea. I hope we're great friends, and I wouldn't want that to change because we had complicated it with more feelings than there are." She sincerely hoped that he hadn't fallen too hard.

"Fair enough," he said a little too quickly. "I hoped you might be able to feel more for me as I think I do for you, but I understand. It's early days." He shrugged.

"I really do want you to be my friend, though, and I'm so grateful for your support," added Jen. She was at a bit of a loss to know what else to say.

Shortly after, he headed for the door.

"Keep in touch, Greg. This has been one whole sorry mess for us both."

She reached up to kiss his cheek, feeling wretched for being unable to reciprocate.

After he had left, she had time to ponder. It had helped to clarify her feelings for Christopher. Waiting another couple of days to be certain, she rang him.

"I'm ringing you, but I don't really know what to say, now," she said.

"Why don't you come round for lunch tomorrow? We'll have a picnic in the garden. It's such a beautiful day today, and I think it's due to be set like this for several more. Charlie is really looking forward to seeing you again." Then he added, "And so am I."

The following day, Jen arrived at Christopher's at half past eleven, in time to help prepare the meal. She chopped vegetables and made some sandwiches, emptied the crisps into a bowl and opened some packets of child-friendly picnic snacks. Christopher opened a bottle of chilled Sancerre and found two glasses. He found a box of fruit juice for Charlie.

He spread a blanket on the lawn under a sunshade and there were a couple of chairs too. The garden was not huge and around one corner there was a bed of shrubs and some summer bedding plants, adding a little colour. Jen was happy to sit on the rug with Charlie, and so they camped down and started their meal.

"This is a treat," Jen said, indicating her glass of wine. "I don't usually go for anything so special."

Charlie helped himself to food, but he was restrained in the amount that he took and he remembered all his pleases and thank-yous.

"Have you got enough, there, Charlie?" Jen asked him.

"Daddy always says I can have some more but I can't put it back," he responded.

"That's very wise and so true," she agreed. Turning to Christopher, she added, "He is such a credit to you."

"We do our best, don't we, Charlie?"

Charlie nodded his response.

Having finished and cleared away the remains, both the adults washed and dried the few dishes. Charlie had an ice-lolly from the freezer, but Jen declined.

"I've already eaten a lot more than I would normally at lunchtime."

Charlie went back outside, and Christopher and Jen followed. She flopped down onto the rug and feeling completely at ease, she lay on her back. Christopher sat beside her and then lay down too. They stayed like that for a while without speaking. Charlie was playing nearby on the grass with some of his cars and a plastic garage that made a variety of noises.

"I think the battery may run out soon." Christopher laughed. "Hopefully. He seems to have a lot of noisy toys."

As they lay soaking up the sun, Jen felt sleepy, but it wasn't possible to doze off with Charlie chattering. She was warm and relaxed with the sun and after-effects of two glasses of wine. Then she felt Christopher's hand creep across the space between them and he took hold of hers.

He turned his head and said, "Is that okay?"

"Yes, it is," she answered decisively. "I've been miserable for too long. It's not just since Mike left but for months before that too."

She could hear a blackbird singing its heart out, and when she squinted up she saw that it was sitting on the gable end of the house. It was one of the sounds of summer and so redolent of good times.

The rest of the afternoon passed pleasantly. Jen played with Charlie while Christopher made coffee. When he brought it out on a tray, they sat in the easy chairs and sipped it, nibbling biscuits, too.

When it was time for Jen to go, she offered her face for a repeat performance of the kiss she had experienced before. This time, though, it was lingering and full of meaning. She felt Christopher's tongue exploring tentatively as he took a strand of her hair and brushed it gently away from her face.

"I think I better go," she whispered, "or I may find it too difficult."

There were several dates after that gloriously relaxed afternoon. On one occasion, Christopher's mum came for the evening and they went to the pictures. Afterwards, they went to the American-Italian restaurant. It wasn't particularly upmarket, but it was stress-free and tranquil. They had chattered and laughed all through the meal. Another time they took Charlie back to the country park and fed the ducks, played on the swings and walked around the lake, holding hands and then swinging Charlie between them.

As time passed, Jen began to miss Christopher on the days that she didn't see him, and she missed Charlie's chatter. Charlie seemed to relate to her with a naturalness that charmed her. He often asked her to read his bedtime story, or to get a bowl of cereal for him beforehand.

Jen was very aware that she could be playing with fire. It wouldn't be fair to toy with Christopher's emotions, never mind those of Charlie. After all, he had already lost his mother. If he became too reliant upon her and she disappeared, that would be intolerably reckless of her. As a result, Jen felt she was holding a little back from them both. Christopher seemed to sense this and didn't push her. However, the time came when she knew she couldn't prevaricate much longer. She recognised that she was placing a great responsibility on Christopher and she understood that he was finding it increasingly difficult.

"I know I said I wouldn't push you," he said one Friday evening in late autumn, "and I won't. The fact is I'd really like you to stay one night. I'm sure you know that. I want you. I want to lie all night by your side. I want to wake up with you beside me. I understand that maybe you can't trust me after what has happened to you, but I think I said once before I'm a one girl guy. I know that I love you, Jen. I have for a long, long time, long before you and Mike split up."

This was a revelation to Jen. "What do you mean?" she asked. "How long?"

"Now I understand that it's pretty much since after you visited Charlie in hospital," he answered.

"But what about Sally?" Jen probed.

"I was attracted to her and I realised I was ready to explore a relationship again, but it wasn't meant to be with her. As I said before, I am grateful to her. She helped me to understand what I really wanted," he said. "I want to help you find peace again, and in time, we shall. I love you, Jen."

Jen looked at him for several long seconds. She knew here was a genuine man; one to whom she was very attracted. She missed him when they were not together. She found herself wanting to tell him all about each day, even the minor events. Did she love him? Did she trust him? She had begun to rely on his steadfastness. She thought she trusted him, but still she couldn't bring herself to say those three little words. Could she commit to him?

It was early days for her, but then she found herself saying, "Yes. Yes, I want to be with you. Shall I come tomorrow afternoon and stay over?"

"I will take care of you," Christopher responded and he kissed her gently.

# CHAPTER 27

Saturday dawned and Jen stretched luxuriantly in bed, immediately aware of the promise of the day ahead.

"Well, Fudge, this is it, for better, for worse," she said to her cat. The irony of her words was not lost on Jen, but they seemed appropriate for the new start upon which she was embarking. Then suddenly she felt nervous. "What shall I take to wear?" she asked Fudge. "My pyjamas are real passion killers. They won't set the tone at all. I think I better nip into town."

She decided to go to the department store where she had bought the new bedding several weeks before. Eventually, she found what she was looking for; something not too slinky but definitely not 'practical' either. She had chosen a pale cream nightdress with fine straps. The hem was just above her knees.

Maybe she wouldn't need it at all, she thought, feeling her heart thumping and heat rising up her neck.

It was early afternoon as she drove home. Jen was very aware that she had only a little time to collect herself. She was planning what she needed to do before driving to meet Christopher at his house. She must leave poor young Fudge some food and check the water bowl. She considered which bag to take and what to pack. Her thoughts flowed on and on, and so she was nearly at the house before she realised there was another car parked in her normal spot. It was Mike. 'Bloody Hell' was mild compared to what she was thinking. Now of all times. She could see the back of his head. He was sitting in the car, presumably waiting for her to return.

She pulled up behind him and, collecting her bags, she opened the car door. Before she had one leg out, he was beside her. She could tell immediately that something was very wrong. He looked completely dishevelled, having not shaved. His clothes looked rumpled and his normally immaculate hair was mussed and even longer than normal. It was several weeks since they'd had contact.

"Whatever's the matter?" she asked.

"Oh, Jen, I need you. I have some awful news. I don't know who else to tell. Please let me in so I can explain. I don't know what to do."

Jen hurried up the path and opened the door. She led the way into the living room, angry that her plans were being so disrupted. She dropped her bags onto the sofa. Not sitting and not offering the ubiquitous coffee, she turned to him, frowning. "Well?" She was feeling uncharitable. *He's not staying long*, she thought.

"The doctor thinks I've got cancer," he said, putting his hands up to either side of his head.

"What?" Jen said somewhat loudly. Then instantly she was sorry and asked, "Why would he think that? Where are we talking about?"

"I went to see him last week because it's been not quite right going to the toilet. It takes ages to get started and..." He hesitated and took a deep breath. "And when I, you know, ejaculate. I gave a blood sample and the results came through. Apparently it measures some type of protein and the reading was too high by far."

"So you're talking prostate," Jen said.

"He didn't say I have got it, but he thinks I should have some further tests. I'm using that private healthcare thing, so I've got an appointment at the hospital on Monday morning. I think they do more examinations and maybe take a biopsy. Hell, Jen, what's going to happen?"

Despite all this drama, Jen was desperately aware of passing time and getting panicky.

Mike continued, "Jen, *please* can you come with me on Monday? I don't want anyone else. I'm really scared."

"I'm sure I've read that prostate cancer can be really slow growing, and you must have got into the system in good time. That's a big positive. Anyway, it might not be what you think. You're awfully young for that. Look, Mike, I've got to make a phone call and then we'll sit and sort out what needs to be done," Jen said.

As she left the room, she found her phone in her pocket and started looking for Christopher's number as she climbed the stairs. This was certainly a call to which she didn't want Mike to be privy. Her heart was thumping as she listened to the ringing tone.

"Hello," Jen heard Christopher say.

"Christopher, it's Jen."

"I know, I recognised your number. Is something wrong?"

"Mike's here," she said

"Oh!" came the non-committal response.

"There's a big problem. He thinks he's got a cancer. He's been to the doctor and had a blood test. Christopher, he's really scared and upset. I don't know what to do," Jen said, feeling dreadful.

"You think you should stay with him, don't you?" Christopher asked. "I guess that's what you should do," he added. He didn't sound very pleased at all, and Jen understood why.

"I'm so, so sorry," Jen said with tears springing to her eyes. "This is not what I want at all, for any of us,"

"Of course not," Christopher volunteered. "You have to stay there. Ring me when you know what's happening. Jen, I love you. I understand this, believe me," he added.

"Thank you," she whispered, not trusting her voice.

As she rang off, she thought, *Of course he understands. He's been through all this with his wife.*

She returned to the living room where Mike was sitting with his head in his hands. As he looked up, there were tears spiking his lashes. She immediately went to his side and put her arms around him. After all, they had once loved each other a lot.

"I'll have to phone Sheila Bagley. Remember, she's the deputy head at school. I'll tell her I need Monday off. It'll be the first time I've ever had a day off, so there shouldn't be any problem."

"Jen, can I stay here?" Mike pleaded.

Jen hesitated, but then she said, "You can stay." Then after a pause, she added, "But in the spare room."

"Of course," Mike responded reasonably. "I need to go and get some stuff from Alex's."

"I'm popping up the road to see Pat while you are gone," Jen said. She desperately needed her friend's good counsel. "Use your key, if I'm not back." She knew he still had it because she had been considering asking him to return it.

"I suppose that's who you were just phoning," said Mike, and Jen did nothing to disabuse him of that idea. She couldn't possibly explain to Mike what had been about to happen when he rolled up. She saw him out and told him to drive carefully.

As soon as he had gone, Jen threw on a jacket and almost ran up the road. Just as she rang the bell, the door opened and Doug was standing there. She had seen him since his return to the family home, but she was no longer at ease with him and she sensed he knew this.

"Hello, Jen," he said. "I'm just on my way out with the boys, but Pat's here. I assume it's her you want to see. Come on, you two, hurry up," he called, turning into the hallway, leaving Jen to follow him. "Jen's here, Pat," he shouted up the stairs.

Pat came down the stairs with a smile. "What's the latest?" she asked when they were alone.

Jen explained all that had happened, confessing that she had been going to spend the night at Christopher's.

To her great relief, Pat was typically prosaic and in her straightforward way she said, "I wondered what was taking you so long to get to that stage."

Jen smiled at this response. Then she embarked on the facts of Mike's arrival and the reason for that.

"Well," said Pat, "that's ironic."

"What do you mean?" asked Jen.

"Ha! He who lives by the sword shall…" But she didn't finish the well-known saying. Instead she said, "Sorry, that's uncalled for. I didn't mean to be so cynical. It's actually dreadful news and I'm really sorry."

They discussed possible outcomes and what might happen at the hospital.

"Have you looked it up on the internet?"

"No, not yet," Jen responded. "This has all happened within the last hour. It's a real rollercoaster. I was just planning my first ever affair and feeling nervous and excited, and then this happens. I can't let Mike do this by himself, though, can I?"

"No, you can't, but it doesn't need to come between you and Christopher either. And by the way, it's not an affair. You might still be married, but you're not cheating on anyone."

"I don't know, I really don't know." Jen bent her head under the weight of it all.

She left shortly after and only felt marginally less confused and upset. It had helped to share the events with Pat, and she had been gratified to hear Pat's response to her developing relationship with Christopher. However, the problems were still all there.

When she arrived home, her husband still had not returned and she was just about to telephone Christopher again when Mike's car drew up and he climbed out to retrieve a rucksack from the back seat. She replaced her phone in her pocket. She would phone him later, in the privacy of her bedroom.

Instead she went to look up Sheila's number in her school diary. Sheila was typically affable when Jen explained the reason for her request, despite the difficulties it would cause.

"Of course you must go," she said volubly.

# CHAPTER 28

Saturday evening was dreadful, with both Jen and Mike avoiding the subject of his possible illness and watching total rubbish on television, trying to be as normal as possible. Jen tossed and turned all night.

On Sunday morning, before she got up, Jen telephoned Christopher. She had been desperately wanting to speak to him but dreading the conversation. How disappointed she'd been the day before. She knew how upset he would have been, too. She hoped he wasn't disillusioned or cross with her.

"It's me," she said when he answered the phone.

She imagined him lying in bed, or maybe he was in the kitchen, getting Charlie's breakfast ready. Then she heard a little voice in the background and what sounded like the television.

"Turn it down a bit, Charlie," she heard Christopher say. Then he spoke into the phone. "Hi, how are you doing?" he asked.

"Oh, Christopher, I'm so sorry, I truly am. I just can't leave him with this."

"Hey, I understand. Of all the people you know, I must be the one who understands best, don't you think? I've been there, remember."

As she lay in bed with the phone to her ear, she put her other hand to her forehead and tears sprang to her eyes. "I'm so lucky to have found you," she said.

"Where's Mike now?" Christopher asked, and Jen sensed he was trying to sound casual.

"He's in the spare room. He asked if he could stay. He was practically crying and very frightened, so I said he could stay, but he has to sleep in there," she reassured.

"I miss you," Christopher whispered. "What happens next?"

"He has a hospital appointment tomorrow. I've got the day off work to go with him."

"Do you know what that involves, what the next steps are?"

"No, I thought I might look it up on the internet so we know what to expect. The doctor said something about a biopsy."

"Will you let me know what happens?"

"Of course I shall. I'll ring you in the evening."

"Take care, Jen. You know I love you."

"I know you do, thank you." Jen really felt she should say it too but something held her back. She wasn't sure if it was because she wasn't yet sure enough or whether she didn't want to lead Christopher up some dead-end path.

She lay still after finishing the call and couldn't summon the energy to get up and face another day of misery with Mike or revisit her feelings for Christopher. Eventually, she gave herself a sharp talking-to and told herself to stop being pathetic. It was just that she was *so* tired. Dragging herself up and coming out of the bathroom, Jen threw on jeans and a jumper. She couldn't be bothered to use the hairdryer so, tugging a brush through her wet hair, she mooched downstairs and put the kettle on. Mike had yet to appear but she got two mugs down and made to get on with the day.

Sometime later, he walked in looking tired too. The day was wet and windy. Jen had some school work that she needed to do and so she was determined to get on with it, regardless of Mike being there.

She found it hard to concentrate. Staring at the wall, she reflected on how far she had come. She was no longer frightened of upsetting Mike and was prepared to do her own thing. She had compromised enough. Now, although she needed to support him through this, she couldn't help thinking of the previous week when Christopher had come to her house for lunch and brought Charlie. She had explained that she must do a little work, but they'd still come early. They had played in the garden and then in the living room while she had got on with it, then she'd got lunch ready. Christopher had understood that she'd needed to do it and was content just to be around. Charlie had brought some toys with him, and he and his dad had made a complicated set-up on the living room floor, which involved cushions and ramps and cars and animals.

Now, as Jen got on with her work, Mike put on the television and was flicking aimlessly through the channels. She felt slightly resentful of his presence, if she was honest. Having been on her own for several months, she found accommodating his needs more difficult. As she got on with her work, she gradually managed to shut out the background distraction until he spoke directly to her. She turned to see what he was referring to and saw that he had one of Charlie's toy cars in his hand.

"Who does this belong to?" He held it up.

"I had some friends round the other day, for lunch. It's one of the little boy's toy cars," Jen answered evasively.

"Oh, who was that?" Mike persisted.

Jen decided to be open. "It was Christopher Mayhew and his son Charlie." She tried not to sound belligerent.

"I see," Mike said, somewhat coldly.

"I don't think you do," she responded. "They came for lunch. Nothing could happen with a six-year-old in attendance, could it? They're my friends."

She was really tempted to add, *Besides, it's nothing to do with you*, but she refrained. With a lot more unsaid, she returned to her work.

Mike eventually sighed, turned off the television and said that he was going round to the paper shop. He asked if there was anything Jen wanted, but she declined and he went out. As the door closed, she breathed a large sigh and realised it was with relief.

Monday eventually came. Mike's appointment was at one thirty and it would take half an hour, at least, to get to the hospital. The information had said it was alright to eat, so they had an early light lunch. Mike was pacing and eager to be off. Jen felt sorry for his distress, so she drove.

It was the large regional hospital. On arrival, they found out where they had to go and headed up the stairs and along corridors to the correct department.

Jen remembered the last time she had been here. It seemed an age ago that Charlie had been here and so poorly, considering how well he was now and how much had happened to Jen since then. He had regular monitoring appointments, but he was quite healed and just as lively and enquiring as before.

Mike and Jen found the right place, and having registered their attendance they sat down to wait. Jen had a book on her phone, but she felt awkward reading while Mike was next to her, staring unseeingly into the space around him. She made an attempt at conversation but quickly realised it was not the way forward, so they both sat quietly and waited. Eventually, Mike was called in.

"Shall I wait here, or do you want me to come in?"

"You better wait, I suppose," he answered. "If I need you, will you come?"

"Of course," she smiled at him. "It'll be fine. You'll cope well."

It seemed an age before she was called into the room. The doctor who greeted her seemed very pleasant and indicated a chair. Mike was in a hospital gown and sitting self-consciously and awkwardly beside her.

"Hello, Mrs Lucas," Mr Wakefield, the consultant, began. "I've done an examination of your husband, and I've just been explaining to him the procedure that I am about to perform. Firstly, we need to send him across for a scan. Then I'm going to do a biopsy of the prostate. It is very simple and should only feel mildly uncomfortable, but it would be better if he didn't drive or go to work for a day or two. I'm just checking that you can take Mr Lucas home and be with him for the rest of the day. I'm doing this now because I've just done a small internal examination which we call a DRE, and I think it would be advisable to pursue the investigations to be sure we know what we are dealing with. It's only a local anaesthetic, and he'll need to rest here for about half an hour afterwards." Mr Wakefield paused to let this information sink into Jen's mind.

She looked across at Mike and raised her eyebrows. "Are you okay?"

He nodded his response.

"Do you have any questions, Mrs Lucas?" the consultant asked.

"When might the results of this biopsy be ready?"

"It should only take a few days. We'll ring as well as write so that, should it be necessary, you can make a further appointment to discuss different types of treatments that are available and we can get underway. I must stress, though, that there is usually no urgency to make a decision about that, as this is not normally an aggressive disease. It may not be necessary at all, of course, but we need to be sure. Yes?"

"Mmm, of course," Jen murmured. "Do you want me to stay?" she asked, unsure of the protocol.

"No, that won't be necessary," Mr Wakefield reassured her. "My nurse here will call you when we're done, and you can sit with Mr Lucas until it's time to go."

Jen nodded and gave Mike a kiss on his cheek before she left the room. She wanted to be supportive and understanding of his anxiety.

Again, Jen sat in the waiting area and tried to calm her thoughts and her racing heart. She had looked up information on the internet. There were loads of good websites, so she knew roughly what was happening. The trouble with limited understanding was that you tended to think about worst-case scenarios, and so she had wanted to be more aware than that.

Eventually, she got the call to go and find Mike. He was looking a bit pale but gave her a smile and said that he was fine. "It was more uncomfortable than painful. I need to wait around now to make sure everything is okay before we leave. I'm glad it's over with, but I'm glad you made me look at those websites. At least I knew a little of what's involved and what to expect."

"We'll be away from here soon," Jen said reassuringly. "We'll go home and have a restoring cup of tea, and I've got some cake in the cupboard too." She knew that was a small and meaningless recompense, but she was at a bit of a loss to know what to say and do. "Sorry," she added. "I'm useless at this."

"Thank you so much for being here, Jen. I don't know how I would be managing without you." He reached across and took her hand.

Jen let her hand rest in his for several minutes, and then fished in her handbag with the excuse of looking for a tissue. She felt suddenly disorientated.

After half an hour, the smiling nurse returned and took them into a side room. The necessary leaflets were given and information exchanged to ensure Mike was fit to leave and knew of after-effects to expect over the next few days, so that he wouldn't panic if he saw some blood spotting. Jen linked her arm through his and together they headed for the door and down the long corridor to find the lift.

That evening, as she had promised, Jen telephoned Christopher to explain what had happened during the day. She reassured him that although Mike was staying, he was in the spare room, and she asked if she could call around after school the next day. She was anxious to see him and Charlie, and she felt she needed to re-establish their rapport.

It felt weird having Mike living with her again. Jen reminded herself that it was only for a few days, and she couldn't help planning how she would broach this with Mike if it didn't look like he was leaving.

# CHAPTER 29

The following day, Jen saw Christopher on the playground before school started. He waved to her and came across just as the whistle blew.

"Will I still see you later?" he asked.

"Yes, please," Jen answered. "It won't be until about five o'clock, though, if that's okay. I've a short meeting after school that I really can't put off."

"Of course, that's fine."

Christopher gave her hand a surreptitious squeeze but didn't kiss her in full view of the playground. Jen guessed that he knew she was not ready for that level of advertisement yet.

That evening, Charlie had gone to tea with a friend, and so it was just the two of them. Jen really felt she loved Charlie, but it was a relief that he was absent on this occasion. Under the circumstances, she welcomed the opportunity to have more of an in-depth discussion with his dad and spend some time just being together.

When she arrived, Christopher enfolded her in his arms but then released her with no further passion.

"I found the visit to the hospital really difficult. I felt so useless," Jen said.

"It's almost harder for the one who's not ill," Christopher added. "There's nothing you can do but be there and be supportive."

"Mike was really scared. I encouraged him to find out some facts. I thought it was better to know what might be afoot. Do you think that was correct, or do you think I should have left him to find out everything from the doctors at the hospital?" Jen asked.

"I know about all those feelings of uncertainty and being unable to help ease the fear and pain too." Christopher placed his arm around her shoulders as they sat together.

Jen leaned her head on his shoulder. "You've been exactly where I am now," she said. "Well, no, not exactly. Mike and I are no longer together. It was worse for you. Mia was your wife in every way."

Christopher said that he wished intensely that all would turn out better for Mike than it had for his wife. Jen knew he meant it too.

"Research and early discovery are the keys. Hopefully Mike has sought medical support in good time, if it does turn out to be that. I'm sure it's usually not an aggressive form. *Please* let me know how things go, Jen," he implored. "I hope that you still want to pursue our relationship once this is all behind you."

She guessed that he was panicking that she would forgive Mike again.

He took her hand between his. She looked down at his strong brown fingers, then up into his green eyes and saw all the anxiety and pain there. "I know I've found a genuine love again, and I don't want to contemplate what will happen if you return to him." His eyes were sincere as they searched her face for some reciprocated emotion. "I know I shouldn't put this pressure upon you, Jen," he said desperately. Then he paused for a few seconds before he spoke again. "I need to fight for you now. I love you so much."

"Oh, Christopher," Jen whispered and tears started to seep silently from under her lashes and slide down her cheeks. But still she couldn't say those words to him.

His arms came around her, enveloping her in their security, and she hid her face in the crook between his shoulder and neck. They sat for some minutes while Jen wept out her misery and anxiety. Having unleashed all her pent-up fears and uncertainties, the tempest slowly passed. She continued to snuffle for some time and just leaned into his warmth.

Eventually, she was able to pull away from him. Looking up, she gave a watery smile and said, "Sorry."

"Listen, Jen," he said, taking her shoulders and holding her firmly until she looked up. "I completely understand how you feel and the place you're in currently. I love you and will wait until you're ready, whenever that may be. Yes, I want you, more than anything. It would be so tempting to rush upstairs right now, but I want to make our first time together special. I, of all people, know what's happening right now and I'll support you in any way I can."

With that, he kissed her gently and released her. She kissed him back and turned to look for her bag to find a tissue. *What an amazing man*, she thought. *Why can't I just go to him? Mike and I have a long history, and we were once good friends. Perhaps I owe him my loyalty, especially now. But he's let me down so badly.*

The next few days passed quite quickly for Jen because she was so busy at work. She was not home particularly early each day, having classroom preparation, meetings and a thousand other things to do. Mike was back at work, and most evenings when she arrived home he was already there and had started to prepare the evening meal. Towards the end of that first week after they had attended hospital, he welcomed her with a glass of wine when she arrived home.

"What's this in aid of?"

"Oh, nothing in particular. You seem tired, that's all. You haven't got to do more work tonight, have you? I thought we could watch that film on TV and just chill out a bit. I feel as if I've done nothing but wait for these damn results. We both need something to take our minds off things, don't we?"

"Mike, you need to go back to Alex's soon," Jen blurted out. "This is foolish. Neither of us knows where we are at the moment."

"Please let me stay until I get the results, Jen." Mike looked at her searchingly. "I really need you."

She put down her glass and looked at him. "You can stay until then, but that's all. I can't live like this."

"It doesn't have to be like this," Mike said.

"It does at the moment," she answered. "Until we know what's happening and what we want."

"I know what I want," he said with meaning in his eyes.

Jen turned away. "Don't!" she said. "Let's just wait for these results first."

During the following week, one morning they were each still in bed when they both heard the metallic rattle of the letterbox. They met on the landing, but Mike was first down the stairs. Bending down, he picked up the letters and shuffled through them until he came to the white A5 envelope. He grimaced and waved it at Jen, having seen the printed logo.

He sighed and said, "This would appear to be it. I don't want to open it."

Jen came down to stand by his side and put her hand on his arm. "Go on, do it quickly."

Mike's follow-up appointment to see the consultant was soon arranged, and again Jen was able to take the afternoon off work to accompany him. He was no less scared, because it was now confirmed that he had cancer.

Again they waited in the same area, and eventually the nurse with the smile and the robust figure called them in. This time, Mike wanted Jen to go with him.

"I may not take it all in," he said.

Mr Wakefield was sitting on the end of his desk with a folder open in his hands. His glasses were perched halfway down his nose and he looked over them as they entered. He introduced the Macmillan nurse who was already in the room. Taking off his spectacles, he waved them at the two chairs nearby and smiled as both Jen and Mike sat. He moved his chair to the end of the desk. He was doing his best to remove some formality and make them feel easy, Jen thought briefly.

"Now, don't look so worried. This is perfectly treatable these days," he said. "We grade what we have found on the Gleason scale. This goes from 2 to 10 and we can put yours at 7. Now we also do a 'staging'. This describes where your cancer is and whether it has progressed further. We see yours as a T2b. This means that it can be felt in more than half of one side of the lobes but not in both sides of the gland. So that's not too bad. Also, you get a zero for the N stage, which is to do with lymph nodes, and a zero for the M stage, which is to do with other parts of the body. This all might sound a bit technical, but it means that you are at an intermediate risk."

"That sounds a bit scary," Mike said. "I'd rather have heard low risk."

"It's not as bad as you think," Mr Wakefield assured Mike. "There are several courses of treatment, and I'm going to outline those for you. You don't need to decide now. It's best if you go away, have a chat with Mrs Lucas and then we'll crack on with what we think is best, yes?"

"Mmm," Mike responded quietly.

"Now, we can offer 'watchful waiting', which basically means we do nothing but monitor the growth."

Mike looked across at Jen and grimaced.

"However, I have to say, since you are such a strapping young lad and you've measured a 7, that may not be the best thing. It's extremely rare for this condition to be diagnosed this young. Now, if you were eighty years old, since this type of cancer is very slow growing, chances are you'd be dead of something else long before, so 'watchful waiting' might be the best answer."

Mr Wakefield went on to describe different treatments involving implanting low dose longer term radioactive seeds that would destroy the diseased cells, freezing and thawing treatment, high dose radiation for a few minutes at a time into the prostate gland, as well as external radiation or even surgery to remove the gland altogether.

Jen's mind was buzzing. It seemed a lot to take in, and she was glad that she and Mike could discuss each method at home later. They were able to ask Mr Wakefield about possible side effects and also the advantages and disadvantages. He was so positive throughout and clearly said that Mike's chances of a full recovery were very good. Following treatment, they would monitor him annually to ensure no return of the disease.

"Now, before we do any of that, you'll have a hormone injection. This will reduce the testosterone, because the cancer will feed on that. You may experience some hot flushes and a bit of weight gain in certain unexpected places. Then you'll need one of those every three months." The consultant looked at Jen and grinned. "Now, if you were older, Mrs Lucas, you'd know what I'm talking about. Most women find that part quite amusing, since it's what they go through at menopause. Now, of course, that will affect your abilities in the bedroom. Mrs

Lucas, you must be prepared for lack of libido and infertility with your husband, I'm afraid. We can offer counselling, of course. I know you have no children yet."

By the time they had finished, both Jen and Mike were exhausted. The Macmillan nurse gave them lots of paperwork to take home and discuss. She was lovely and gave them her phone number too.

"There's a lot to take in, and sometimes it's harder for relatives than the patient. You may forget what you've been told, so if it's not in these leaflets do ring me," she said.

Once they were home again, they both collapsed onto the sofa and sat in complete silence. Eventually, Jen looked at Mike.

"Tea?"

He nodded his response, so she rose and went into the kitchen to fill and switch on the kettle. He followed her and as she turned, he drew her into his arms. For some moments, Jen felt warm inside his embrace. The smell of him was familiar and her head fitted comfortably against his shoulder. Then she gained her senses and pulled away, turning again to gather mugs, milk and to pour the hot water.

# CHAPTER 30

The weeks passed. After Christmas, Mike started on his treatment. They had opted for Low Dose Radiation brachytherapy, which involved the implantation of rice-like 'seeds' to which the radiation could be added. The chances of problems with incontinence or impotence were reduced, and in one so young that seemed a good thing. Also, the seeds were aimed very precisely at the problem. Jen had accompanied Mike for his implant treatment appointment. He had gone as a day patient. He'd had a general anaesthetic, but he was fit to come home at the end of the day and had gone back to work only a few days later. After this initial therapy, Mike also returned to his friend Alex's house.

Perversely, Jen missed him to start with. They had not shared a bedroom at all, but having another person around in the evenings was becoming a habit again. She continued to see Christopher and Charlie. Occasionally, at weekends, she stayed to eat. As the weather got milder again, they went out for the afternoon and did things that entertained the young lad. They all got on so well. Christopher steadfastly avoided the question of Jen staying the night, and she felt very contented and relaxed with him.

During the following weeks, once or twice, Mike had stayed in the spare room for a couple of days if he had been feeling rough. Mr Wakefield, the consultant, seemed to be pleased and very positive about progress, though.

Spring passed quickly and summer approached. Jen was becoming more and more convinced that she was being unfair to Christopher. She had been on the brink of being in his life fully, and then all the medical complications with Mike had arisen and, despite their differences, she had felt loyal to her husband. She really didn't know if this was misplaced or not, but she couldn't leave him to cope with all that on his own. In the meantime, Christopher had been extraordinary in his patience and understanding. He frequently reminded her that he understood, having been through the same thing with his wife, although that had not turned out happily at all. He persisted in trying to reassure her that he would wait for her to be ready to accept his full love and partnership. Equally, Mike was starting to press her to allow him back into her life fully. The time had come for her to make a life-changing decision.

Jen had been to see her mum and dad. While they had genuinely loved Mike, they had been very disappointed by his behaviour because of the impact it had had on Jen. She knew, however, they would agree with whatever she decided and support her wholeheartedly. They had met Christopher and Charlie, and they thought Charlie was adorable and could see that Christopher was a dependable man who was also a devoted and caring dad. They liked his humanity, patience and good humour and understood that they were characteristics good for Jen. They had seen that he and Jen got on very well and that she was more than fond of Charlie. However, they were also unsure if having a child from another marriage in her life was an added complication.

Pat had been so supportive over the last few months as well. She understood Jen's dilemma. After all, she had her own troubles with Doug and she knew what it was like to feel let down and yet to develop a shell in order to survive that battering to the self-esteem.

The end of July came and school finished for the long summer holidays. Having got some energy back after a long and busy term, Jen made up her mind to sort out her life once and for all.

She picked up the phone to speak to Mike with some trepidation and arranged to meet him.

"When shall I come round?" He had hope in his voice, she thought.

"Let's meet away from here somewhere," Jen said. "Maybe at the park, neutral territory."

Times and days were sorted out, and she couldn't help starting to imagine how this fateful meeting would go. She hadn't told Christopher of this arrangement. She honestly couldn't decide which way to spring, and she didn't want to raise his hopes unnecessarily.

Jen parked her car and arrived early enough to walk through the park and gather her confidence. Now was the time. She could see Mike at the far side of the lake. She could have been feeling a sense of power over these two men in her life; two people who wanted her. This was not how she felt at all. She was feeling confusion and chaos. Pat had assured her that she would know what decision to make when she arrived and met Mike. She desperately hoped so. As she neared the bench and Mike, she could see he was pacing around. She took some deep breaths to calm her nerves.

"Hello." She waved uncertainly as she approached.

He had not seen her before, eyes to the ground as he patrolled. "Hi," he responded awkwardly. "Do you want to sit or walk?"

"Let's sit for a while," Jen answered, unsure of the strength in her legs at this moment. "How are you doing since we last saw each other?"

"Really well," he said. "The radiation should be well on its way now and finishing soon. I don't seem to have had any major side-effects. I'm due for another scan in a few weeks to verify the tumours are gone. Mr Wakefield said they'll keep me under regular review for several years. I feel so lucky, Jen." There was an awkward pause. "What have you been up to?"

Both of them, Jen realised, were putting off the crux of their discussion. "Well, we've broken up from school, now, of course," she answered desultorily. She realised she would have to take the initiative. "Mike, we have to make some decisions. We can't go on like this indefinitely. Apart from anything, Alex won't want you there forever."

He jumped in straight away. "No, he won't. In fact, he asked me the other day what was happening. Jen, I could come back home."

"I don't know." She looked down at her hands in her lap. "I'm not sure I'm the same person, and I'm not sure that you really want to be with me either."

"I do. You know I'm really sorry for what happened," Mike said. "I don't know why it did."

"I shall still need to do my school work. I shall still be earning more than you. None of that has changed."

"It doesn't matter," he insisted.

"But you promised me it was over, and then you still went back for more with Diana," Jen said quietly.

"I know, but that wasn't for long anyway," Mike responded.

"What? What do you mean, it wasn't for long anyway?"

"Well, it wasn't. It only lasted a couple of weeks that second time."

Jen could feel herself getting angry now. "Oh, well, that's alright then, I suppose," she said acerbically.

"It wasn't meaningful. It wasn't important," Mike justified.

"It wasn't important to you, maybe, but you made promises to me when we got married. You broke those. Then you lied to me *again* after making a further promise." Jen sighed deeply and stood. It was her turn to pace now. "Wasn't important, you just said. It was critically important to me. Mike, if you think it wasn't important, then I don't think we can carry on." There, she had said it.

All of a sudden, things became distinct, crystal clear. She remembered his attitude previously when he'd seemed to carry on as normal. He had said it was over and had brushed it all from his mind as if it had never happened. She turned to face him. He was still sitting on the bench, looking up at her with a slightly puzzled frown.

"Mike, I'm not taking you back. I'm not going to because I'm not giving you permission to lie to me and betray my trust like that. I'm not going to carry on as if it didn't matter and let you believe that's how it was."

He looked at her, completely flabbergasted. "I thought you wanted to meet so that I could come home," he said after several long moments.

"If I let you come home, it means I'm allowing you to think it's been okay to treat me as you have and to see what you have done as unimportant," she said quietly. Her anger had evaporated as quickly as it had come. Now she was feeling succinct in her thoughts and understood what there was between them.

"So there's no such thing as forgiveness in your world," he said bitterly.

"It's not a case of forgiveness," she said. "It's a case of us not feeling or understanding the same thing about marriage and what it means. Mike, that's it, I'm sorry. Well, actually, no I'm not. I'm just not consenting to marriage on those terms."

"I see," he said, though she doubted he did. "That's it, then?"

"That's it, Mike," she murmured.

The magnitude of this moment did not elude Jen. She was sad, very sad. She had felt disappointment, failure and crushing loss over the last few months. However, more recently she had begun to see that this was not of her making but rather a fundamental difference between them in the meaning of this relationship. They had to part. As she stood in front of him, she saw dawning realisation on his face that she meant what she said and that she truly would not be changing her mind.

"That's it, then," he said again, standing. "What do I say? See you around?"

"We'll need to sort out the house and our stuff," she said forlornly. "Ring me soon, and we'll meet to discuss it. It'll have to go on the market and we'll just split it all, I suppose."

With that, he kissed her cheek and without further words he turned and left. Jen sat down again, heavily this time. With her hands in her lap, she took a deep breath and lowered her head. She stayed without moving for some time.

Finally, she raised her eyes to the sky and closing them she sat silently, calming her pounding heart. There were the distant sounds of children who were oblivious to all but their fun; she heard the birds singing for the joy of a sunny day; she smelled the balminess of the turf around her. Eventually, she became aware of herself. Rising up from the seat, she slowly moved towards the car park.

When Jen reached the house that, in a short while, would no longer be her home, she sat in the car for a moment. Then she went indoors because she didn't know what else she could or should do. She had an awful feeling of anti-climax following all the emotion of the last few hours. She dumped her bag and keys and just mooched around from one room to another. Then there was a ring at the front door. She jumped and immediately her heart started thumping.

*Oh no, not Mike, please no*, she thought. She edged towards the door and saw, from the outline through the glass, that it was Pat. Momentarily she sagged against the wall, such was her relief.

"I'm afraid I was watching out of the window and saw the car. I've been a veritable curtain tweaker. The boys are out the back on the field with their bikes, so they may join us quite soon, but I had to come and see you, Jen." She smiled and reached out to touch Jen's arm.

"Come in, Pat." Jen held the door wider.

"If you want to be on your own and have some space, that's fine. I can go away now that I've seen you're in one piece," Pat said.

"No, it's fine. In fact, I'm pleased to see you — a bit of normality," Jen added. "I need to start sharing my news, although there are some key people I need to tell as well as you, so it's probably better if you keep it to yourself until I've spoken to Mum and Dad and Christopher, particularly."

"I see." Pat waited to hear more.

"We're parting," Jen announced. "I can't let myself settle for his form of marriage. It may never happen again, but I can't take that risk. He said that the second time he went back to her it wasn't important, but it was." The more she thought about that, the more incredulous she became at Mike's reaction.

"Okay, on one level it was just a quick roll in the sack. But it tells me that, basically, I'm not as significant in his life as I need to be."

"I said to you once before that I think Doug is more meaningful to Doug than I am," said Pat. "Some people are more self-centred than others. They reckon two out of three men will cheat at some time. It seems we've got the two." She shrugged.

"You've found a way to cope with it, but I can't," Jen said.

"I've got two children, but you haven't yet," Pat added. "Maybe that's the difference. I'm not saying it's better to stay together for the sake of them like in the old days, but if I can accommodate my own feelings so that Doug and I chug along together in some fashion, without bickering and bringing up old wounds, then I hope that's better for them."

"You are some special kind of person, Pat," Jen said.

With that, they heard young voices at the door. Answering the knock, Jen found Pat's two lads looking pink and warm.

"Come in, you two," she said. "You look hot and thirsty. Would you like a drink and a biscuit?"

"Yes, please!"

"Mmm, thanks, Jen."

They pounded up the hall and into the kitchen. Joe flung his arms around his mum's waist and Ben went to wash his hands at the sink. Jen was pleased to have the occupation of getting them refreshments and the normality of youngsters around her. They munched the biscuits and downed the squash with the exuberance of the young.

"Thanks, Jen," they said in unison.

"We're going back up to the field, Mum," said Ben.

"Alright," said Pat. "Don't go away without saying, though."

After the bright breeziness of the youngsters, Jen was beginning to feel more positive than she had done for a very long time.

"So the next big question is Christopher, and of course Charlie," stated Pat.

"Yes, but I can devote my full attention to them now," Jen said. "I do think I've been quite selfish over the last few months, but Christopher kept saying he understood and that I must get sorted with Mike's illness first. It's just been too difficult somehow while Mike was undergoing treatment and staying here for such a lot of the time. I knew I couldn't abandon him through all that. I can't believe how lucky I am that Christopher has been so patient and understanding. I hope I haven't asked too much of him with all this waiting."

"What's the latest on Mike's medical stuff?" Pat asked.

Jen told her the positive news as she understood it.

"He's very fortunate," Pat responded. "Treatments nowadays are incredible, but it's a good thing, too, that he went to the doctor early." After a pause, she continued, "Well, I better gather up the boys and head for home to sort out lunch. You've got plenty to do and think about. I'm so glad you got back safely and are okay. I've been thinking about you since you left this morning."

"Once again, I have to thank you, Pat," Jen said. "We'll talk soon."

That night, Jen was dog-tired but couldn't sleep. So many things were going around and around in her head. She needed a day or two to understand her own emotions and to be sure of what she needed to say to Christopher before she saw him again. Perhaps she should remain on her own and not be in a relationship at all.

Then she thought of him, and her tummy flipped and her heart pounded just a little faster. She missed him as she lay thinking about his gentleness, the good fun they had, his kindness and understanding, his patience, his green eyes and his strong arms, his hands.

It came to her with a flash. She loved him. She sat bolt upright. She loved him. Without thinking, she leaped out of bed and ran downstairs. She must be mad.

*I love him.*

She threw on her coat over her nightdress and stuffed her feet into her sandals.

*I love him.*

The front door banged behind her. Running out to the car in the dark, she wrapped her coat around her and tied the belt, not stopping to zip it up. She managed to drive somehow. Parking the car outside Christopher's house, she ran up the path to his front door. She knocked breathlessly. The door opened and he stood there looking tousled and bewildered then worried.

"I love you." At long last Jen uttered those words that she had been unable to say and threw herself into Christopher's arms, relaxing as they closed around her. "I love you," she whispered.

# A NOTE TO THE READER

Hello Dear Reader,

I started writing this book many, many years ago and my author mother was very encouraging, urging me to finish it. However, two young children and a full-time job got in the way and it rested in a drawer for almost thirty years!

After I took early retirement and we moved to France, where I needed something to do other than taming a wild garden, I dug the book out, dusted it off, and finished writing it.

It's had a change of title, some major re-writing, and some superb editing from the Sapere Book team since then, so I hope you find it a satisfying read. I have written several books following this one, which all goes to prove it's never too late to give this wonderful activity a try, should you be contemplating it.

If you did enjoy *Reaching For Tomorrow*, perhaps you might leave a brief review on **Amazon** or **Goodreads**. It doesn't need to be long; a couple of sentences will more than suffice. It will inform readers when choosing a book and would be a huge boost to this author. Thank you.

If you would like to know more about my writing, my website is **www.rosrendleauthor.co.uk**. Here you can also **sign up for my newsletter** where I often offer free gifts and timely access and information about forthcoming books. I'd love to hear from you, my dear reader, and you are able to chat with me via **Facebook** or via **Twitter.**

Of course, none of this would be possible without the incredible skill of the team at Sapere Books, so it's with huge grateful thanks to each of them for transforming my scribblings into this book.

Thank you, again, and I hope we will meet again soon through the pages of one of my other books.

Ros Rendle

**Sapere Books** is an exciting new publisher of brilliant fiction and popular history.

To find out more about our latest releases and our monthly bargain books visit our website:
**saperebooks.com**